the alchvhybium bet

the multiverse of benji and jay
book one

Pip Dolyn

Cover Illustration by Kay Claire

Layout by Pip Dolyn

Edited by Lindsey Middlemiss

ISBN-13 979-8-9921463-3-2

Sub-Radio, "Dimension"
0:33 - 1:00

preface

This book contains consensual sexual scenes that are not intended for underage readers.

Benji is a trans man who has chosen not to undergo medical transition and often uses female biological terms when describing his anatomy. Please take care if this will upset you.

This book proudly contains:

- queer, trans and non-binary characters
- magical realism
- calico cats
- no TERFs
- a university setting
- explicit sex between two enthusiastically consenting adults where one partner takes a dominant role and the other is submissive
- a loving relationship between two queer men
- chocolate chip cookies and beverages
- teleportation sigils
- a magical tea house

- a conservation/aquarium with magical creatures
- use of female anatomical slang to describe a trans man's body, by and about him
- brief mention of a possibly closeted trans woman in the past, in a secret relationship with another woman, bringing up their biological child as a ward

pronunciation guide

Alchvhybium - alk-VIH-bee-umm

Vhakyllus - VA-kill-iss

Cassiopeial - cass-ee-oh-peel

Scarpial - scar-pee-ull

Aural - arr-uhl

Talminkum - Tal-mink-umm

Relkarbrium - Rell-car-bree-umm

Lancidpod - lan-sid-pod

Vasjhyllid - Vass-ill-idd

Fjona - Fee-own-uh

Taaques - Talk-kwess

Belherston - Bell-err-stun

Octojel - ock-toe-gel

Subluceo - Sub-loose-EE-oh

Algaefish - al-gay-fish

Rootent - Roo-tent

Amhritran - Ahm-ritt-tran

prologue

An Apartment in New York City

"BABE?" Jay Byrd walked through the door to the small apartment he shared with his husband, Benji.

"In here," Benji Rollins called from the left of the entry way. A prolonged hiss and some clanging that sounded like it shouldn't be happening had Jay rushing to the much too small galley-style kitchen, where he found his husband waving a towel in the direction of a shiny espresso machine. An espresso machine that *hadn't* been in the kitchen when Jay left for work this morning.

"Err, when did we get that?" Jay asked.

"I won it in a work giveaway thing." Benji shrugged. "I can't figure it out though. It keeps yelling at me. Olive hissed at it when I took it out of the box and, when it started hissing back, she ran into the bedroom."

Their calico princess had always been a little skittish since before they adopted her from the rescue. The staff said she didn't like people, but she warmed right up to Jay and Benji. Jay practically had to drag Benji away from cuddling with her. They got about three blocks, with Benji turning around every seven steps saying he was going to go back for her, before Jay had to admit that he had already put in the adoption application and a deposit to hold her for them. Jay smiled at the memory of Benji picking him up in the middle of the walkway and spinning them around before dragging him towards the nearest pet supply store. Jay went willingly. He always followed Benji willingly. The spontaneity kept Jay from collapsing in on himself and he was grateful for a partner who embraced life the way Benji did.

Jay took the kitchen towel from his husband and pecked him on the cheek before scooting him out of the cramped room and taking over. His muscle memory from the years spent as a barista in college took over and by the time Benji had fished Olive out from under their bed and settled on the couch, Jay had prepared two expert-level lattes made just how they liked them. He placed them on the coffee table and snuggled up to his big warm bear of a husband and their calico princess.

"Hi baby," Jay rubbed his face in Olive's fur and her purring went into overdrive.

"How come I don't get that kind of affection?" Benji joked.

Jay scooted down and rubbed his face against Benji's belly. Benji imitated Olive, purring, and Jay cackled with laughter, setting them both off giggling, Jay's head bouncing on Benji's stomach. After their giggles settled, Benji began playing with Jay's hair, in between bouts of petting Olive, and Jay felt tension seep from his body.

"Aside from winning my new favorite appliance, how was your day, babe?" Jay asked.

His husband started talking about his latest project and all the complications he was encountering. Jay closed his eyes and listened, surrounded by his man and their cat.

chapter **one**

Vhakyllus University

BENJI ROLLINS HAD A PROBLEM. It was obvious to his colleagues, it was obvious to his students, it was obvious to the janitor who kept walking in on him pacing and scribbling on chalkboards at 2 am in the transmutation professors' lounge at Vhakyllus University. Benji Rollins had a problem, and it seemed like nobody could help.

He dismissed his last class of the day from their alchemical transmutation lecture and decided to go to the library, yet again, to do more research. With his leather satchel nearly bursting at the seams with the abundance of papers and notebooks unceremoniously stuffed in it, he turned left out of the lecture hall and headed down the corridor.

Benji had been working on the same problem for the last three weeks, and he was no closer to finding out about the ancient element than he had been when the vision of his next sculpture appeared in a dream. The first stop, as it had been for the past six visits, was to the reference desk to see if anyone had luck tracking down *anything*. At this point, he didn't care if it was a passing reference in some early century tome, he just needed to know that what he dreamed was real and eventually attainable.

"Hi," Benji greeted the young magician at the desk. Their open textbook with accompanying notebook suggested they were a student worker and the solid green lanyard holding their school ID confirmed it. "I'm wondering if the reference librarians left me anything. I'm Professor Rollins."

"Umm, ID please?" The student held out their hand and Benji passed over his own school ID with its patterned purple-and-orange lanyard denoting he was a tenured professor. The student closed their eyes and Benji felt the familiar pulse of an illusion detection spell radiate down their arms and over Benji.

"Checks out, Professor," the student said as they handed his ID back to him. They turned to the computer and started typing. After a minute, they frowned and gave him the bad news. "Looks like there's a note that just says there's been nothing found." Benji bit back the curse on his tongue. If there was nothing in the university's extensive library, he'd have to admit defeat and then his latest piece would literally be sent back to the drawing board.

He thanked the student and was turning around to leave when the student spoke up. "Have you asked Jay at all?"

"Jay? Who's that?" Benji questioned, turning back to the student.

"Jay is the new research librarian for the archives. This note says you've been working with Zephyr and they're great and all for most stuff, but if you're looking for something they can't find, you'd be better off asking Jay."

"Why didn't—" Benji cut himself off. Airing his grievance about why the reference librarian he was working with didn't ask the archivist about this ancient material would only put the poor student in an awkward situation and he didn't want to do that. He had a reputation of being the cool, easy-going professor, but this project had him stressed.

The student, whose name he probably should have asked by now, picked at their nails and finished his question for him. "Why didn't Zephyr just ask Jay to help? Well, there's a bit of a rivalry between the two, but you didn't hear that from me. Anyways, Jay is in today. If you go up to the Cassiopeial floor, you'll find the archives, and Jay, in room Scarpial B."

"Thank you." Benji leaned over the desk to read the name on the student's tag. "Felix. Thank you, Felix."

"Anytime, Professor." Felix winked at him and then went back to their studies.

Benji turned and headed deeper into the library. It would be faster to take the teleport, but he needed to work out some of his tension and frustration, so Benji opted to ascend the grand spiral staircase to the Cassiopeial floor, five stories above.

chapter **two**

JAY LOOKED at the blinking ink on the paper and cursed out his colleague. "Damnit Zephyr."

Sure, he wasn't the most social of librarians, but he was used to spending his days in solitude due to the nature of his work, so trying to make friends was difficult and he was awkward and a bit eccentric. He *thought* the weird facts he had catalogued in his brain would endear him to other reference librarians, but you correct one person in front of the wrong person *one time*, and they harbor a grudge for you years later. He might not have applied to work at Vhakyllus if he had known his old college rival would also be taking a position there. Alas, he couldn't dwell on that now. The flashing message from Felix said that someone was on their way up to ask him a question Zephyr couldn't answer.

No surprise there. Jay wouldn't snark out loud, but that didn't mean he couldn't internally gripe while he waited for his new visitor.

Instead of dwelling on the petty feud, Jay tidied up his already immaculate desktop and wondered what subject he would be challenged on today. He hoped it was something more original than the last three requests he'd gotten for historical uses of armor and weapon conjuration in battles. Those requests didn't need to go through him as they were readily available in the main section of the library, but he assumed it was Zephyr fucking with him, wasting his time by sending those students to him.

A light knock on the door of Scarpial B jolted Jay out of his thoughts and he looked up to see a gorgeous, if a little haggard, bear of a man walk towards him. Unless he was pursuing a late-in-life education or a continuation of a post-graduate degree, Jay assumed he must be a professor because he looked too old to be a student.

"Hi," the haggard visitor greeted him, with a smile that made Jay's insides tingle and squirm.

"How can I help you?" Jay asked shortly. He really didn't want to waste either of their time if this was another Zephyr prank.

The stranger's smile faltered a little. Jay inwardly scolded himself for his curtness. "Sorry, that was rude. I've just had a number of recent visitors being improperly sent my way. Let me try that again. Hello, welcome to the archives, what can I help you find today?"

The stranger's eyes softened a little, but Jay didn't feel pitied, he weirdly felt seen and it made him uncomfortable. He didn't like to be perceived. It's half the reason he loved working in the archives.

"I'm looking for help identifying an ancient element and am out of luck with your colleagues at the main reference desk." He set a camel-colored leather satchel on Jay's desk and started digging through the disorganized mess inside. Jay didn't want to dwell on the chaos in front of him, so he took the time to look over the man. He had an orange-and-purple lanyard holding a school ID draped over his neck, so Jay discerned that his initial impression was correct: this man was a professor, Professor Benji Rollins to be exact. His clothes were a little disheveled—there were some wrinkles in his baggy linen floral overshirt and the black T-shirt underneath held splattered stains that matched those on his frayed boot cut jeans and black combat-style boots. A single star cluster earring dangled from his left ear. Jay wasn't sure if he was only wearing one because he lost the other or because it was a deliberate fashion choice.

Jay stepped back out of the way of Professor Rollins's arm a fraction of a second before it flung out of the bag with a notebook clutched in his hand. Rollins enthusiastically set the notebook on top of the contents spilling out of the satchel and rifled through the pages until he found a detailed and labeled drawing unlike anything Jay had ever seen. That fascinated him. Gifted with a photographic memory, Jay didn't often encounter things he'd never seen in his thirty-seven years in this universe. He pulled his glasses off the bust they rested on to recharge and put them on.

"Are you okay if I record this?" Jay asked.

The professor nodded, so Jay powered the glasses on and primed them to record.

"Intriguing," Jay said, leaning closer to inspect the drawing.

"Thanks. It came to me in a dream," Professor Rollins admitted. "I'm an artist and part of my magic is being able to create the sculptures and pieces I see in dreams. This piece is pretty much all figured out, but I'm missing the final element. It's this one here." He pointed to a light, translucent blue core flowing through the center of the abstract sketch.

"What is it?" Jay asked.

"I was hoping you could tell me." Professor Rollins

grimaced at Jay. "All I know is what came to me in the dream. It's a translucent pale blue element with some sort of liquid core that's constantly in motion. Have you ever come across anything like that before?"

The professor actually crossed his fingers as he looked hopefully at Jay, who found the gesture strangely cute and endearing. He mentally shook off the distraction and started to process the information through his mental catalogue. He fired up the crystals on the side of his glasses and thought through his index to see where certain keywords would cross reference. The initial search in gems brought up nothing, but Jay refused to give up.

"A quick look into my personal database doesn't bring up anything, but that doesn't mean it doesn't exist. I just did a quick mental search through gems, so we've ruled that out."

"How extensive is your database?"

"Quite. It's built off my own photographic memory and the archives here. If the answer is here, I'll find it."

"And if it's not?" Rollins asks.

"If I can't find an answer for you, I'll have to rethink my career."

"Don't do that, I'm sure you're good at what you do. You come highly recommended after all." The professor winked. *Was he flirting?* Jay was thrown off guard. No one ever flirted with him.

"How about this," Rollins continued in a lower voice that hit Jay like velvet. "If you can't find it, you buy me coffee from Jack's."

"And if I do find it?" Jay asked, in a voice much more sultry than he was used to or even intended. *Was he flirting back? That can't be right.*

"*When* you do find it, I'll buy you coffee from Jack's. Or

the beverage of your choice. I don't know if you drink coffee."

Jay wasn't sure what was compelling about this virtual stranger, but he wanted to know more about the professor and his sculpture with the mystery element.

"You're on, Professor," he agreed.

chapter three

BENJI WAS HALFWAY BACK to the art department when he realized he never gave Jay a way to contact him when he found something, and Benji was confident that Jay would find something. He had been too mesmerized by the librarian's heterochromatic eyes and the way his glasses accentuated the colors. Benji was sure that the colors of hazel and blue would feature in one of his dreams soon. He was already imagining formulas to recreate the right patina on bronze that would replicate the color variations in Jay's left eye. As for the blue, Benji was certain that when they figured out what the mystery element was, he'd be at a perfect starting point for that eye as well.

Benji hung his satchel from the antique coat rack that held his leather jacket. He pulled out the sketchbook that he had let Jay examine with those glasses before he left and studied the construction plans again. The sculpture was constructed with an onyx half that would be tricky on its own to replicate due to the varying finishes on the facets. The other side, a patinaed copper that was getting swallowed up by the onyx would be easier, and Benji had a good foundation for it, ready to be sculpted. The biggest issue was going to be this blue mystery element. In his dream, Benji had observed it between the onyx and the copper representing some sort of chemical reaction between the two substances. It mostly flowed between them, but there were a few chunks that arched off like sparks.

Benji initially thought the onyx and copper would have a reaction like that when they were matched up, but he couldn't replicate the reaction in any of his tests. He talked to the magic sciences department and the other alchemists on staff, but no one could figure out the element. It was actually the janitor who encouraged him to talk to the reference librarians, after finding him in that spiral one night. If this worked out, Benji would have to buy that janitor a ridiculously nice gift.

Benji got to work pulling out his stock of copper paper and found the right agent that would add the correct patina to the final look. He'd have to be careful with how it was constructed because the patina was applied in a gradient across the sculpture, with a heavier application covering the form closest to the overlap. He looked over at the larger and more detailed version of the piece that was on the chalkboard next to his workstation. He'd already calculated the copper and onyx formulas but didn't want to start anything until he had found the new element so he could be sure the construction wouldn't have any catastrophic reactions.

He had just finished a 1:10 scale version of the copper portion with the two closest patinas to the seam when he noticed the pulsing glow of the old message relay system. It rarely got used anymore as most people used cell phones these days, but the university kept it running in case of emergencies. Benji walked over to the glowing clipboard and found one thing written:

Iced Vanilla Matcha with Almond Milk, Large

Laughter burst up from Benji's chest. It had barely been two hours since he left the library and it seemed like Jay had already found something. Benji had to stop himself from rushing back over there, so he placed an online order from Jack's Magic Beans, the on-campus coffee shop for a large iced vanilla matcha with almond milk, his usual caramel hot chocolate with a double shot of espresso, and two of the large chocolate chip cookies. He hoped Jay didn't have an issue with gluten.

Benji cleaned up his studio in record time. The only thing that remained on his workbench when he left was the drying paper sculpture and it was already starting to transform into the patinaed copper of its final form. He also gave himself a once over with a simple cleaning charm to remove the art splatter and generally tidy up his messy appearance.

Magic is so cool. The thought crossed Benji's mind as he set off to pick up his order from the café.

chapter **four**

"ONE LARGE, iced vanilla matcha with almond milk, as promised." Professor Rollins barged into room Scarpial B and presented the beverage to Jay with a flourish that wasn't present the last time he had been in this room. The excitement was brimming off him and Jay could practically see his aura glowing. It was a shade between orange and yellow, similar to a goldenrod crayon.

"And a chocolate chip cookie fresh from the oven. It's still warm." The professor giddily placed Jay's favorite cookie down next to the beverage. He gaped up at the strange visitor.

"That's my favorite. How did you know?" Jay asked.

"I made an educated deduction, and by that, I mean I guessed and hoped you didn't have a gluten sensitivity or allergy."

"Thank you, Professor Rollins. That was quite kind of you."

"Are you kidding? It was the least I could do. I've been working on this problem for months and you seem to have gotten something for me in a matter of hours." The professor nearly tossed his beverage all over Jay's desk in his exuberance. "And please, call me Benji. Professor Rollins makes me sound old and stuffy. I'm generally not as frazzled and uptight as I came across earlier today."

Benji. Jay let the name roll around in his mouth and it tasted like a buttery coffee—delicious and thick, a bold flavor with the right amount of sweetness. It was comfortable and Jay was unsettled by the draw he felt to the man before him.

He reached into his hoodie's front pocket and pulled out the small stone he rubbed when he was working through problems. Benji was certainly a problem as far as Jay was concerned.

"Okay, Benji then. Thank you for the beverage and the cookie." Playing with the stone in one hand allowed him to regain some semblance of control over his social anxiety. He took a sip of the beverage and scarfed down half of the cookie before putting them both to the side and pulling out the small tome he had discovered in his research.

Benji straightened up in his chair and placed his own beverage and cookie next to Jay's.

"Is that it?" he asked. Jay grinned. Time to show off.

"Yes. I believe I have the answer you're looking for. The element you described is one that no longer exists in nature and hasn't been around for nearly 4000 years. It's described here as a rare metal with a thin glass-like pale blue layer over an ever-moving molten core."

"That's it." Jay could see the shock on Benji's face and it translated to his aura. He continued with his presentation.

"It's called Alchvhybium."

"Alk-vibbium," Benji echoed.

"Yes, here." Jay turned the book around to show Benji, who eyed the ancient text in front of him with reverence.

Jay sat in silence watching Benji study the pages of the

tome that Jay had marked. Benji's lips were moving in silence as he read the words and Jay once again took time to study his new colleague. His appearance looked fresher than it had when they first met a couple of hours ago.

"This is amazing, Jay. You're a legend." Benji beamed at the librarian who in turn met him with a quizzical gaze.

"A legend? Hardly. I just did what any research librarian worth their salt would do."

"Well, considering I worked with Zephyr for two months and she didn't find anything, you're a legend in my book."

Jay didn't mean to insult his colleague, but he also wasn't too concerned about it coming across that way either. Zephyr's grievance with him shouldn't extend to the greater Vhakyllus University community. She could have come to him sooner. She was intimately familiar with his cataloguing system as she had used it quite a few times before Jay's weirdness got to be too much for her.

Jay didn't exactly know how to respond, so he just smiled and flipped his stone between his fingers.

"So does this answer all of your questions or did you need help finding something else?"

Benji looked over the text again and pursed his lips. They were plump and Jay had the sudden urge to find out how they tasted. Before he lost control of his impulses, Benji put the book down and stepped back from the desk.

"I do actually have a question," he stated.

Jay just looked at him waiting for him to continue.

"How do I make it?"

chapter five

"I'M SORRY, how do you what?"

Benji watched as the librarian's face scrunched up in confusion, and he had to bite back a smile at how adorable he found it.

"Make it. It's the missing part of my sculpture. I need to make it." Benji attempted to clarify himself, but Jay's face was communicating that he wasn't doing so effectively. "It'll be easier if I show you. Come on."

He reached out and took hold of Jay's hand, pulling him toward the door out of the archive. Jay hesitated only long enough to grab his matcha and credential badge before they were out the door. Benji took them to the center of the floor, where the library's teleportation circle was inlaid into the floor. Both men tapped their feet to activate the sigil and found themselves in the library's entrance.

Benji was impatient, but he had learned through watching too many first-year students to wait until the sigil stopped glowing before attempting to leave its border. He watched Jay take a sip of his drink and finally the sigil's gold glow faded. Benji stepped out at a quicker pace than his usual walking stride but he wasn't running like he had been up on the Cassiopeal floor. Despite the hurried pace, Jay easily stayed in step with him.

"Where are we going?" Jay asked when they were around the corner from the transmutation department.

"My office. Well, it's less of an office and more of a studio at the moment," Benji rapidly explained as he hurried around the corner, desperate to show Jay what he meant. "Regardless, it's where I work." Benji stopped at his door and started moving his hands in the familiar rhythm to unlock it. When he finished, the solid cherry slab slid open to reveal his mostly clean workspace and the model of his piece that he had left on the workbench.

"So you teach transmutation?" Jay asked as he looked around at the space and the collection of books that paled in comparison to what Jay was used to working with.

"Yes," Benji confidently stated. "My specialty is alchemical transmutation. My thesis revolved around the mix of chemicals and magic to replicate different materials and patinas. The application I teach is rooted in my own art, but it has practical applications for construction and everyday manufacturing."

"Impressive," Jay admitted. Usually when Benji started talking about his research and thesis, people quickly lost interest, but he didn't get that vibe from Jay, who seemed genuinely impressed.

Benji moved over to his sculpture and Jay abandoned his perusal of Benji's measly bookshelf to look at the winding piece of half-transformed paper sculpture.

"How does it work?" Jay asked, getting close to the piece, one hand rubbing a stone that he had pulled out of his hoodie pocket.

"Well, my process starts with paper. I collect recyclable paper and draw sigils on them. After they've been imbued with the correct base properties, I shred it up and blend it with water to create a pulp. While it's in the pulp stage, I drain a good amount of the water and then mix in blends of chemical to enhance the base properties or add additional properties. When everything is mixed well, I let it sit and absorb. It starts to activate in this stage and then I have a limited amount of time to sculpt it before it will lose its malleability and begin to transform to the final look."

Jay didn't speak, continuing his inspection of the demo piece. Benji started to get antsy, shifting from foot to foot.

When he couldn't take it anymore, Benji broke the silence. "This is just a scale model of the final piece. I just wanted to make sure it was working correctly."

"If this is a scale, and you only have a limited time to sculpt before it transmutates, how do you replicate it on a large scale?"

"Good question. With this base copper material, or with many other metals, I'm able to include a sigil to slow the reaction and get more time to work with the material. I don't usually do that when I'm creating the scale model though because I'm usually able to sculpt what I need before the drying begins. It's taken a lot of trial and error though. At least my sculpting is based on paper, so the old sketches didn't go to waste at all."

Jay chuckled and bit his bottom lip. "Reduce, reuse, recycle." His heterochromatic eyes met Benji's self-perceived less impressive brown ones and Benji's breath hitched, swallowing the saliva filling his mouth so he wouldn't choke. *This man is stunning. His eyes, his messy sandy brown curls, the dimples make his appearance when he smiles or laughs*—Benji was struck with the desire to know whether Jay's peach-colored lips tasted like the fruit they share a color with.

They stared into each other's eyes for what felt like a

millennia, Benji hypnotized by the cosmos in Jay's eyes. He only looked away when they were interrupted by a knock at the door.

"Hey Professor Benji, I—" The voice cut off. Both men turned to see Beryl, Benji's teaching assistant, at the door with a stack of papers in their hands. "Sorry, I didn't mean to interrupt. Just wanted to drop off these papers. They're all graded and ready for your final review."

"No, it's fine Beryl. Thank you for these." Benji stepped forward to take the stack and his assistant gave him a look, conveying that they knew he was a little smitten with his new colleague. Benji cleared his throat. "Beryl, this is Jay. He's the new research librarian for the archives. He's helping me with my mystery element."

"Hi, well, I'll leave you two to your *research*," Beryl said and grinned.

"I should probably get back to the library." Jay's quiet voice was like a yell to Benji and he knew he didn't want their interaction to end. His brain began racing, desperately trying to come up with an excuse that would convince Jay to stay longer or think of some reason to see him again.

"Wait! Before you go..." Benji interrupted before Jay could make it all the way to the door. Jay's well-worn canvas high tops turned so he was facing the professor.

"Yes?" Jay asked, with a hint of hope in his question.

"Can you help me figure out the formula? Or should I bet that you can't?"

"Oh, I'm pretty sure I can." Jay's dimples reemerged with the tease.

"Hmm, I don't know about that." Benji took a couple steps closer to Jay. Heat and tension filled the short distance between them.

"What will you give me when you lose?" Jay teased, biting his lip again. Benji felt the impulse to reach out and brush his thumb against the spot Jay habitually bit. He put his hands in the pockets of his jeans and started rocking back and forth on the heels of his boots to alleviate the need to move.

"*If* I lose, I will take you out to dinner. Anywhere you want to go," Benji promised.

"You're on, Benji," Jay said, promptly turning around to leave, his hips swaying a little more than usual as he sauntered away.

chapter six

JAY FELT like he was floating all the way back to Scarpial B. He had to look down a few times to confirm his feet were making contact with the ground. *That's the strange thing about magic*, he pondered, *it feeds off of your intentions*, so with his head in the clouds, it wouldn't be strange if his feet tried to get him there. Thankfully he was inside a building the whole way back.

The only thing that could dampen his mood was waiting for him back to the entrance to his archives—Zephyr Skybolt.

"To what do I owe the displeasure, Archivist Skybolt?" he asked flatly.

"I'm here about Professor Rollins's account," his colleague responded. Her voice grated on his nerves: she played up the nasal affectation in order to fit in with a more pretentious crowd during grad school. For some reason they all sounded that way, as if the stuffier they sounded, the stuffier their opinions and thoughts would be.

Jay looked at Zephyr and waited for her to go on. When it was apparent that she was waiting for an apology or explanation, Jay sighed and resumed the conversation if only to get it over with quicker.

"What about Professor Rollin's account, Zephyr? Can you please be specific and precise? I have an urgent project that requires my attention." Jay scooted around Zephyr, careful not to physically bump into her even though she was twice his size in both stature and aura.

"I'm curious why you felt the need to usurp my position as the lead researcher on his account." Her arms crossed tightly across her broad swimmer's chest. Jay could tell that she still kept up with her training because both her arms and chest were as impressive as they always had been.

"Zeph, I didn't usurp anything. At least not intentionally." Jay could feel a tension headache brewing. "You weren't in and he needed immediate help. He was directed to me after your attempts to help had been unsuccessful. It's Vhakyllus policy and best practice that he's welcome to request assistance from an additional researcher at that point. And again," Jay started playing with his comfort stone, "you were not here."

"I may not have been there that day, but I've been here every time since. It's professional courtesy that you turn over the research and direct him back to me."

Jay balled the stone up in his fist. "You're correct, that would be a courtesy that is often given, but in this case, Professor Rollins expressed his wish to continue working with me, and *that* is what usurps courtesy. The wish of the client outweighs our feelings."

Zephyr vibrated with frustration. She knew that Jay was right. Jay knew that she knew.

"Fine. Enjoy Professor Impossible. His requests are just more and more impossible. I'm sure you'll be begging me to take him back by this time next week."

Before Jay could get in the proverbial last word, Zephyr

turned on her heel and walked off to the other side of the floor. She waved her arms at the door to Scarpial A and it slammed behind her with a force that would have upset every librarian and patron on all seven floors if she hadn't cast a silencing charm.

Jay took a deep breath in, rolled his shoulders and neck to relieve some of the tension, and passively unlocked Scarpial B.

The hum of life greeted him, as did the warmth and smell of vanilla mixed with bibliosmia. He breathed in the essence of the ancient tomes and began his researching ritual. A wave of his hand towards the kitchenette turned on his kettle and his tea began preparing itself. He stepped over to his desk and placed on his glasses.

These glasses weren't just regular readers: they were part of his graduate project. Jay had figured out how to imbue them with magic based on his own photographic memory. Wearing these glasses assisted his eyes, so he was able to avoid straining over long hours. Instead of having to transcribe and organize a filing system, the glasses would help him catalogue where different texts would reliably be sorted. It was synced with his brain, so while it might work well for him, it would be difficult for anyone else to use them reliably without an extensive setup process. But the results were phenomenal. Jay was able to pull up research he encountered over a decade ago, just by thinking about a few keywords, and without the intense fatigue that used to plague his long research sessions. There was also live tracking for each of the books in his archive, so he just had to think about the tome he was looking for and the glasses would guide him to it, something he found particularly helpful when he had assistants reshelving books.

Jay brought up the research he was going through with Alchvhybium. He would need to look for more books on the subject because he had a feeling he'd be working with Benji on this project more than their initial search. At least he hoped that would happen. He had lied to Zephyr earlier when he stated that Benji had expressed his wishes to continue working with Jay instead of her, as Benji hadn't outright stated it to him, but if Jay had taken over as his lead researcher on file, that meant that Benji must have said something to someone.

Jay caught himself smiling at the thought of Benji going through the process of making sure that they would continue to be paired for future projects. A subtle rattling to his right broke him out of his reverie. Jay reached out and settled the tea tray on the sideboard. He waited while the cup filled with a perfectly steeped tea and shot it down. He set the tiny cup back on the tray and got to work.

When the room's lights brightened around him and his stomach started growling, Jay realized he'd been lost in his work for more hours than he could mentally account for. He took off the glasses, sat back in his velvet armchair, and rubbed his eyes. His stomach growled again, angrier than before, and Jay knew he had to give into his hunger. He'd come back to the books after finding food.

chapter seven

BENJI FELT PRETTY glorious this morning. He slipped on his binder and sighed at the relief his back felt. There were days when he loved having breasts, and he certainly loved them being played with during sex, but most days, he was thankful to the binder his friend developed in college and then went on to patent. It started out as a joke, but Willa figured out a way to magically restrict a chest without causing lasting damage. Benji helped her figure out the alchemical component for the fabric, which not only gave him a bit of a windfall when the patent went through, but also gave him binders for life.

He donned his favorite skinny jeans with the patches, a floral shirt that complemented the patterns, and put on some of his favorite rings and jewelry. He planned to check in with Jay again today and hoped that he'd be able to take him out for that dinner soon. He knew it was technically dependent on their bet, but Benji wanted to take Jay out regardless of how his research was going. As much as Benji hoped Jay's success in finding out more about Alchvhybium would give them the opportunity to spend a meal together, he also knew that his soul felt connected to Jay in some way and he would do whatever it took to spend more time with him.

Benji was able to rein in his thoughts enough to give his 101 class a lecture, but while he was proctoring an exam for his 217 class, he let his mind wander. Benji was so far deep in his memory of Jay's elusive smile and warm vanilla scent, mixed with something else that he couldn't place, that he missed the class finishing their exams and exiting the classroom. Beryl shuffled the papers and tapped the stack on the edge of the desk before Benji noticed the empty classroom.

"Wow, Prof, you got it bad," Beryl laughed.

"I do not," Benji defended himself. Beryl's laugh turned into a cackle.

"Look behind you." They pointed at a chalkboard full of different runes and illustrations.

"Oh, you have got to be kidding me," Benji exclaimed with an exasperated sigh. "Well, at least they remembered the fundamentals of the course material."

He maneuvered his hands through the gestures required to clear the board and then turned back to Beryl.

"Sorry Beryl, I've been distracted lately and it's just getting worse." Benji was glad he had the type of relationship with his teaching assistant where admitting his shortcomings was met with understanding instead of prejudice.

"He was very cute. Seemed kinda shy, though."

"Yeah, perhaps. I don't know. Do you ever just feel drawn to people and know that they're meant to play a starring role in your life for years to come?"

"I do," Beryl admitted. "Your auras complemented each other well, and I'm fairly certain he saw it too."

"You think he's an aural?"

"Yup. There's a distinctive shaping to the way an

aural's personal aura surrounds them and it was evident with his."

"Interesting."

"We aurals certainly are." Beryl smirked and placed the test books down on the desk. "So, when are you going to see him again?"

"Soon, I hope. I'm waiting for a message, but I don't know if I can realistically wait that long. My soul has felt like it's been vibrating all morning. I don't think it'll settle until I see him again."

"Yeah, Prof, it has been. I had to send three students out of the room because your aura was pulsing and strobing so intensely they were starting to get headaches."

"Ah, shit. I'm sorry." Benji knew that aurals were more susceptible to magically induced headaches than most and it wasn't easy to concentrate when something like that was practically flashing in front of your face on a good day. Having to take a test while someone's aura was distracting you was near impossible. Benji was glad Beryl was also an aural and knew what to do in those situations.

"Can you note which three were impacted? I want to make sure that I take that into account during grading." It was only fair.

Benji and Beryl sorted through the tests and made a game plan for the grading. Then Beryl picked them all up and shooed Benji off to go check on Jay, before his aura upset everyone in the building.

Benji's aura calmed as he set off. He stopped by Jack's Magic Beans to pick up another iced matcha and a chocolate chip cookie. He wasn't sure if it would be a celebratory offering or a necessary pick-me-up, but either way, he hoped Jay would appreciate it.

Before Benji could enter the library teleportation circle

up to the Cassiopeal floor, he was called over to the desk by the same student who referred him to Jay.

"Hey, Professor Rollins."

"Hi again, Felix," Benji greeted them in return. He hoped Felix missed the glance Benji took at their ID badge.

"How are things going with Jay? Was he able to help you find everything you needed?"

"Jay has been great. He's been everything I needed." Benji hoped that Felix wasn't also an aural.

"I figured he'd be a good match. I need to confess something to you."

Benji softened his look and gestured for Felix to continue.

"I changed your file."

"What does that mean?"

"Well, the library arts dictate that once a lead researcher is assigned to a client, they are supposed to remain with them until both parties agree to part ways or until the client requests a change. I know you weren't having luck with Archivist Skybolt, and the way you and Jay left that day made it obvious that you two would be a better fit, not to mention you've been back to visit a few different times, so I went in and switched your lead researcher. I can change it back—"

"No," Benji objected, louder than he had intended. A couple of librarians lifted their heads up from their desks and glared at him. "No, Felix, that's not necessary," Benji continued more quietly. "You made the right choice. Consider this my formal request to be partnered with Jay. I appreciate you getting that started for me so there isn't any delay, since we've continued working together on this project."

Felix nodded and smiled at Benji who smiled back, then turned and continued up to Jay's floor.

He was outside the door to Scarpial B when he gave himself a once over, made sure the cookie was still warm, and then knocked.

The door opened on its own and Benji entered to find an over-caffeinated and agitated Jay pacing back and forth, having a conversation with the air. His hands were gesticulating around him with two fingers holding the small stone he usually kept in his hoodie pocket.

"Okay, so try Talminkum and Relkarbrium."

Benji waited and then when Jay let out an agonized groan, he put the beverage and cookie down and stepped into Jay's space. Jay stopped his pacing and even though Benji wasn't an aural, he could feel Jay's spirit start to calm.

Jay took off his glasses and set them down on their designated spot on his desk.

"Hi," Benji offered.

"Hi." Jay looked pained when he returned the greeting.

"What's wrong Jay?"

"I can't find it," he admitted.

"Can't find what? Alchvhybium?"

"Yes. It's impossible to track down. I think it's extinct and no one has it, so I was trying to find similar elements that might be able to be combined to create the same properties, but that's just leading me from dead end to dead end. I can't… I haven't… I don't know if I can do this."

Benji felt a pain near his soul as he watched Jay draw up into his oversized hoodie and curl up on the green velvet armchair next to his reference desk. Benji sensed that Jay needed space, but he also felt compelled to stay, so he scooted the goodies over to where Jay could easily reach them and then made himself at home in the leather chair opposite Jay.

After a few minutes, Jay wiped his face and snagged up the still-warm cookie. He took a bite and Benji licked his lips seeing some of the chocolate ooze on the side of Jay's mouth. He wanted to taste him. It. He wanted to taste it. The cookie. Benji mentally shook his thoughts and looked back at his colleague. Nope. He still wanted to taste Jay's lips, chocolate and all.

Benji kept waiting, ignoring the arousal rising to the surface and trying to keep it from overtaking his aura. He started box breathing and counting spines of books, remembering different formulas, and problem-solving basic alchemical equations. When he looked back at Jay, the adorable archivist was smirking at him.

"Do you," Benji started, his voice cracking. He cleared his throat and tried again. "Do you want to go for a walk? Clear your head? It might help."

"Why not." Jay shrugged and stood up. He walked to Benji's side and stuck out his hand. Benji stood up and took it. "Lead the way, Professor."

chapter **eight**

JAY FOLLOWED Benji out of the library, past the alchemy department, all the way to the forest on the edge of campus. Most magical universities were surrounded by ominous woods where various creatures hide with the hope of ambushing unsuspecting voyagers. The woods surrounding Vhakyllus were much more inviting. Sunlight streaked through the trees creating a chiaroscuro shaded pathway. The trees and vegetation were a vibrant verdant green as if a rainstorm had just passed.

The pathway Benji led Jay down was clearly lined by smooth river stones. Jay watched Benji's aura gently ease the further down the path they got. Eventually, they came to a small alcove with a natural driftwood bench. Benji gestured for Jay to sit and then sat down beside him. They weren't touching, but Jay felt Benji's aura reach towards his and looked down to watch as they playfully intermingled. Jay smiled softly as he watched the sunshine color of Benji's aura dance with his cobalt blue, creating a deep green shade where they blended.

"This is one of my favorite spots on campus," Benji started after a few minutes of silence.

"It's very inviting and peaceful," Jay admitted, lifting his gaze from their auras and looking around at the forest surrounding them. A deer grazed on some leaves in the far distance and a rabbit curiously watched the two men before hopping away.

"Here it is."

"What do you mean?" Jay supposed the non-magical nature of the forest was due to Vhakyllus's proximity to the city. Most magical universities were set away from dense populations due to secrecy laws enacted when they were founded. Vhakyllus was a fairly new school in that regard —the first of its kind, open to magic and non-magic students alike. While the students gifted with magical talent made up the majority of the practical application studies, many of the students without magical talent had equivalent studies that benefitted from them learning together. In the medicine program, magical students focused on mastering the incantations and imbuements needed to produce certain magical effects such as wound care, disease detection, and potion ingredients; whereas their non-magical counterparts learned about how to brew potions and work alongside medicinal mages as equal teammates. Groundbreaking studies showed that blending magical and nonmagical practices lead to much greater patient satisfaction as well as more effective diagnostic and treatment practices. Vhakyllus students were pioneers and remained at the forefront of most blended studies.

Jay was brought back from his speculative thoughts on the university's history when Benji let him in on a little secret.

"The forest only looks friendly. When Vhakyllus was founded, it was set as a barrier to keep protestors and anti-magic agitators out. In order to be effective at that, they stocked it with some creatures that would dissuade any trespasser who came across them," Benji admitted diplomatically.

Jay turned and crooked his eyebrow at Benji. "What sort of creatures do you mean? Surely it would be a liability to keep anything too dangerous around. I mean we have rabbits and deer. It's not like Vhakyllus has let lancidpods roam loose." Jay shivered at the thought of encountering a rhinoceros-sized beast with an acidic exoskeleton so potent it deadened the ground the beasts walked on.

Benji didn't meet Jay's eyes.

"Benji… is there a lancidpod in the forest?"

"A herd. But they mostly stay near the pond in the center of the wood."

"A herd?!" Jay jumped up from where he was sitting and started to dart back down the trail when Benji called out.

"They can't cross the border," Benji shouted. Jay turned to see him pointing at the rocks that lined the path. He slowly came back and stood in front of Benji.

"Explain, please," Jay demanded.

"So, when I first got here ten years ago, I was talking with a few professors at one of our luncheons about how we wished there was more of an opportunity to just be outside in nature. The gardening and farming students do a wonderful job of maintaining the fields, but it's hard to walk through there and enjoy it without getting in the way of someone's project or disrupting the balance of some of the different crops in rotation. We took our conversation out to the forest border and started to dream about finding a way to use the resources we had to create something special for the students and staff. A few of us from the alchemy, transmutation, and illusory departments worked together and came up with these."

Benji picked up one of the stones bordering the path

and held it out to Jay. Jay turned it over in his hand and saw that there was a rune embedded in the pattern of the stone on the bottom.

"Illusion came up with the rune that essentially projects what's going on in the forest as harmless non-magical animals just existing in a natural state. I worked with the alchemy team to embed two runes in each stone. We replicated the border containment spell to ensure that none of the creatures can wander onto the path and then we figured out how to enhance and project the spell that the Illusion team came up with, so all the stones work together in one network. Because my work focuses on alchemical transmutation, I also worked with the transmutation team to create the rocks that line the path. It took a good year and a half of work, but we were able to get it done. There's even a paper for it and a few of the professors who helped develop it have gone on to create a program that brings the infrastructure to other magical institutions."

Jay handed the stone back to Benji and contemplated the professor's brilliance. The fact that Benji was an alchemical transmutation professor was impressive enough. Most magic practitioners focused on one branch, but Benji had found a way to blend two of the most technically difficult branches in a way no one had ever accomplished before. That he then took that knowledge and helped develop a cutting-edge practice with three magical branches successfully blending sparked something in the back of Jay's brain. All of a sudden, his mind was whirling with thoughts and he needed to get back to the archives to plot it out.

"Benji, you're brilliant," Jay exclaimed.

He rushed up to the professor, squeezed his arms around him, gave him a quick peck on the cheek, and then rushed off towards the library.

chapter nine

BENJI HADN'T MOVED in half an hour. His hand was still touching his face where Jay's soft lips had pressed against his cheek. It was the briefest moment, but warmth still radiated from the spot. A rustling noise shook Benji out of his reverie and he watched as a couple of birds flitted around the tree's canopy—chasing each other and diving towards the ground, before racing away through the forest.

His footsteps took him back to his office where he grabbed his satchel and set out for home. Like most professors, Benji didn't live on campus, but unlike the majority of his colleagues, he didn't rely on his apartment's teleportation sigil for his daily commute. As long as the weather wasn't out of balance and he wasn't sick or injured, Benji preferred to walk. His walk took him along the edge of the forest towards the northern trail into the city of Vasjhyllid. If he was in a rush, the walk took Benji about twenty minutes from his apartment bordering the city's side of the forest to his office, but Benji enjoyed taking his time, savoring the sights, sounds, and even smells of the landscape.

Today's walk felt different. Benji was certain that the

sounds were louder and exuberant, the air was sweeter, and both suns were shining. A pleasant breeze accompanied him to the edge of campus, and when Benji was back on the forest trail, harmonious birdsong accompanied him to the border. As soon as he reached the trail head, he was greeted by the neighborhood cat, a small calico he had dubbed Fjona. She rubbed between his legs and made it impossible for him to move forward without paying a toll. Benji was prepared for this daily ritual—she had trained him well—and he presented a tiny fish snack as today's offering. Fjona accepted the treat and Benji left her munching on it, fully aware that she would find him later when she wanted his attention.

The sensation of Jay's kiss was finally starting to fade, but the joy on his face at the breakthrough remained engrained in Benji's mind as the evening progressed. At first, he found it comforting, but the longer it remained, the less Benji was able to concentrate on the work he intended to complete. He set aside the stack of tests he was grading and pulled a sketchbook out of his satchel. It fell open to the next available blank page and Benji summoned a pencil. He did his best to turn off his thoughts and let his hand lead. The muscle memory and his brain's memory of Jay's face worked in tandem until Benji had sketched out a rendering of Jay's joy. The one element that escaped him was Jay's eyes. He had been enthralled with their heterochromatic nature since he first saw them, and every time he studied them, he discovered something new, but he still wasn't able to accurately portray them in his sketch.

Benji flipped to the next page and closed his eyes, hoping that denying his sight would help him better recall the gateway to Jay's soul. His hand sketched out a number of shapes but nothing felt correct. The high from earlier had now fully disappeared, replaced with the determination to draw until he made acceptable progress. It was an impulse that only overtook Benji at his most passionate and pivotal moments.

When Benji was finally satisfied with the eye's shape, his hand felt like it was ready to fall off. As if she sensed his need for a distraction, Fjona appeared on the ledge of Benji's third floor apartment window and loudly called to be let in. Despite her status as a neighborhood cat, Benji felt a little responsible for the soft creature. He opened up a new container of food and set it out next to a clean water dish. Fjona let out little chirps as she trotted toward her dinner. Her enthusiasm, and the growl his stomach let out, reminded Benji that he needed to feed himself, too.

Satisfied after eating, Fjona curled up on Benji's lap for their nightly routine of warm cuddles and conversation. Magical familiars were a thing for some magic users, but Benji never had need of one. Fjona wasn't technically a familiar, but she was a welcome companion each evening —she listened while Benji recounted his days and even chimed in some nights. Tonight's story had her a much more active participant than usual.

"And then, he kissed me."

Fjona let out a loud chirp, sounding shocked and excited for her friend.

"I know," Benji exclaimed. He scratched the underside of her chin and allowed himself to settle a bit. "I mean, I like him Fee. He's cute… and seeing him smile is one of the most gorgeous, mind-melting experiences I've ever had. Knowing that I can put that smile there fries my brain. Gods, and his dimple. Did I tell you about that?"

The calico head bumps his hand and he continues. "Well, he has a dimple—just the one—on the right side of his cheek. It's only there when he really smiles or laughs."

Benji realized he was gesticulating widely as he talked, so he channeled his restless energy into stroking Fjona's fur.

"We have this bet, and I'm really excited to lose it, and not just because it will mean that he's found an answer for me, but because losing it means I get to take him out on a date. It's inevitable that we're going out on a date, though. If he loses, that just means he takes me out, and I'd love that too."

Benji sighed and relaxed back into the couch, Fjona's weight keeping him rooted in place.

"Looks like I'm sleeping on the couch tonight, huh girl?" Benji commented, resigned to his fate. After a quick enchantment that left his mouth clean, he reached over and grabbed a pillow, thankful that he'd had the forethought of putting a blanket on his lap before Fjona had got settled.

The early sun's light gently beamed across Benji's face, waking him from another night spent in his living room. Fjona was already gone and, sometime during the night, Benji had grabbed another blanket and reclined into a more comfortable position. The clock on his wall showed that this morning would need to be a little rushed.

Benji made it to his office with enough time to set down the stack of half-graded exams for his afternoon class, check his memo board, and grab the lecture notes for today's 405 class.

After the hour spent discussing the advanced applications of alchemical copper in urban settings, with only a slight tangent into the ethics of using alchemically sourced materials without disclosure, Benji was hoping he'd return to some sort of message from Jay. He had been disappointed not to find anything waiting for him this morning when he got in, but he figured Jay might not have been in as early as he had. Benji unwarded his office and frowned at the memo indicator light still being off. He sighed and sat at his desk to grade the exams.

Finishing up with extra time before he had to deliver and review the exams with his 101 class, Benji decided to bring Jay a pick-me-up. If his silence meant that yesterday's breakthrough hadn't resulted in anything, Benji was sure that Jay would need it.

A quick trip to Jack's it is then.

The after-lunch crowd made his trip longer than he'd hoped, but his watch showed that he had at least an hour, potentially an hour and a half if he took the teleport, before his class would expect him.

Benji knocked at the door for Scarpial B and waited. After a few minutes of no response, he knocked again. The securely closed door unlatched and creaked open. Benji looked around to see if there was anyone messing with him, but when no one made themselves known, he pushed open the door and stepped in.

"Jay," Benji called as loudly as he dared before the door closed behind him.

There was no response. He hesitated just over the threshold. A tug of intuition urged him in the direction of Jay's desk. He took a tentative step toward it, and when no alarms started blaring, he gained confidence in his stride. Rounding the corner of one of the archive's stacks, Benji stopped when he saw him.

Jay's head was resting on his arms, crossed on his desk. His hood had fallen back off his head, revealing curly sandy brown hair cascading over his face. His expression was restful and Benji took a few moments to study the faint line of freckles that had faded over years spent being indoors. Jay was beautiful. Benji almost didn't want to wake him, but he guessed that Jay had spent all night here and his body would really be regretting his choices if he stayed there too long.

Benji reached out and brushed a curl out of Jay's face, tucking it behind his ear. Jay started to stir, his tired eyes still in a dream-like state when he looked up at Benji and whispered.

"You're here."

chapter **ten**

THIS WAS NEW. Jay knew he was dreaming, but this moment felt truly lifelike. He assumed the fact that he could smell the archives had to be due to the fact that he fell asleep there. But Benji in this arena was glorious. He had been glorious in the past dreams Jay'd had about him. But this Benji was the closest to his Benji.

Jay sighed and let the fantasy begin. Much like the other dreams he'd been having over the past two weeks, it began with a touch. This time, Benji was playing with Jay's hair. Jay nuzzled into the touch and maneuvered his head so that Benji's hand was cupping his cheek. It was warm. That made Jay smile. He basked in the touch and his aura started to glow brighter the more comfortable he felt.

Usually, by now, they would be going hot and heavy with physical touch and affection. Sometimes, Jay's dreams began with them in the throes of passionate sex. Jay was surprised that he wasn't upset with the more gentle and intimate pace of this dream. It had been a long time since he'd let anyone close to him in this way, in dreams or real life. His aura dimmed slightly at the realization.

"Jay?" Dream Benji called. His voice was clearer than it usually sounded, almost as if the real Benji was in the room with him right now.

Jay looked up at the man whose hand was still caressing his cheek and smiled. He tilted his face towards Benji's and willed him to meet Jay in a kiss. At least Jay's subconscious knew where to go from there. Benji didn't move closer this time and Jay could feel the pull of consciousness start to tug at his mind.

"No, Benji, don't leave me. Don't go," Jay urged. He fought to stay in the dream longer. He needed to be somewhere he felt free and unreserved. Somewhere he could pursue these feelings without the danger of rejection.

His body tried to fend off the antsy sensation that came whenever he woke up. Usually tearing him away from the dreams only to wake up alone broke his heart a little, but this time, his stirring was eased by a touch.

Jay slowly succumbed to consciousness and as he opened his eyes, he wasn't alone. Benji was there, hand extended by his ear as if he had reached out to comfort Jay in his waking.

"You're here," Jay croaked out. Benji's eyes and soft smile shone with a care that Jay hoped weren't remnants of his Dream Benji.

"I was worried when I didn't hear from you. I wanted to make sure you were okay," Benji admitted. His aura pulsed and met Jay's, almost as if it was checking to make sure that Jay truly was unharmed.

"I'm okay," Jay assured him groggily. He rubbed his eyes and stretched his neck. Jay wasn't quite sure just how long he'd been sleeping in that position, but he needed to move gently to make sure he wouldn't be in lingering pain for the rest of the day. Benji stood back and watched as Jay elongated his neck and moved it around. When Jay looked back at Benji, there was a heat and longing in his eyes that made Jay flush. The only other time Jay had seen that look was in his dreams when Benji was about to devour him. Any lingering sleepiness snapped away and was replaced by a desire that Jay had been tamping down out of professional courtesy.

"I bet I can make your neck feel better," Benji declared.

Jay met his eyes and rose to the challenge. "What are the stakes?"

"Whatever you want," Benji offered.

"Anything?" Jay's cock started to plump as he thought about the possibilities an open-ended offer would allow.

Benji stepped into Jay's personal space and cupped his cheek. Sparks tingled at the contact. The magical energies surging through their auras intensified. Jay forced himself to keep his eyes on Benji's rather than close his eyes and just feel.

"Anything," Benji confirmed, his voice sure and unwavering.

Jay met Benji's confidence with his own. "You're on. Do your worst."

"Oh gorgeous,"—Benji reached out and clasped his hand on the back of Jay's neck—"just you wait."

Jay's breath hitched and he let himself be guided to the leather chair he had for guests. When he sat, Benji walked around behind him and started lightly tapping his fingers up and down Jay's upper back. He gently pressed Jay's head forward and Jay closed his eyes, basking in the touch.

Benji's touches started to deepen, targeting every little ache Jay had been feeling. The massage was everything he needed. The knots in his muscles might be going away, but the sexual tension between them was building with every moment.

As Benji released one particularly tough knot, Jay moaned in pleasure. He felt Benji's hands slip slightly and his aura pulse with desire. Jay tried to push his own desire towards Benji. He knew Benji wasn't an aural, but Jay was practiced enough to be able to release certain emotions so they could be felt by those around him.

He knew it had worked when Benji's hand squeezed the back of his neck. Jay followed the pressure and looked up at Benji.

"I feel better," he admitted. His tongue traced his lips. "What's your prize?"

"Pretty sure you're supposed to be the one choosing," Benji smirked.

Jay stood up and faced Benji. "Oh am I?"

Benji nodded.

"In that case…" Jay stepped into Benji's space, grabbed his shirt by the collar, brought his mouth a breath away from Benji's and whispered, "kiss me."

Benji lunged and covered Jay's mouth with his. Jay's arms slid around Benji's broad back between the layers of his shirts. His hands clung to the fabric of Benji's undershirt as the kiss deepened. The magical sensation that had surged through their auras earlier pulsed with an energy so powerful that the hairs on Jay's arms stood on end. He had never experienced anything like it.

"Benji," he moaned as the other man started kissing his jaw. Jay pressed his body tighter against Benji's, thrusting his hips as he moved. This kiss was taking him apart and he wanted to return the favor.

Jay's hands traveled down Benji's back to cup his ass. He encouraged the professor's hips to thrust against his.

The friction made both men pause before continuing with renewed fervor. Jay started sucking the pulse point on Benji's neck and, hearing the noises he made, Jay wondered what other noises he could coax from him.

"Jay, please," Benji whined. Jay smiled at the desperation Benji's voice portrayed.

chapter eleven

BENJI FELT his knees start to wobble and was grateful when Jay pushed him back against the mahogany desk. With a flick of his hand, Jay magicked away the papers and tomes, clearing the desktop of anything that could get damaged. Benji's hands gripped the edge of the wood and he gasped as Jay's mouth found his pulse point again. He wasn't sure how Jay knew that it was his weak point, but the librarian had homed in on it like it was his favorite book.

The haze of arousal was consuming him and he wanted to make sure Jay was also enjoying their encounter. Benji started to undulate his hips, increasing the friction, and Jay held his ass tighter. Benji could feel Jay's hard cock behind his pants and had the urge to taste him, but he was still stunned by Jay's mouth on his jaw. He moved his hips faster and moaned, unable to verbalize his desires.

"What do you need, pet?" Jay asked.

Benji just whined in response.

Jay squeezed Benji's ass and drew their hips together, grinding to an imaginary song. The rhythmic movement and the way Jay took charge, letting Benji turn off his brain and give his body over to Jay, scratched an itch in Benji's desire.

Jay pulled away and Benji tried to follow him.

"Trust, Benj," Jay ordered him gently. Benji stayed where he was and gripped the desk in an effort to restrain his movement. Jay stepped back and stripped off his hoodie, revealing his lithe body. Benji swallowed as he noticed Jay's jade green shirt ride up and show off a soft stomach—a stomach Benji wanted to lick. He whined and Jay fixed him with a playfully stern expression, the double tone of his eyes piercing Benji to his soul. A relentless desire he had long suppressed burst to the surface of his thoughts. He *needed* to submit. Benji dropped to his knees as Jay approached. He placed his hands on his thighs and waited.

Am I doing this right? Will he want this, too?

Benji's thoughts began to spiral. His gaze was on the ground in front of him. He watched as Jay's feet entered his view and swallowed again. Two fingers reached down and tilted his chin up. He hesitated to meet Jay's eyes, but when he did, he was rewarded with an expression filled with arousal.

"Hello pet," Jay mused. Benji's lips twitched into a smile. "You look so beautiful on your knees for me."

Benji shivered with the praise. His eyes flicked down to the bulge in Jay's pants. Jay chuckled as he moved one of his hands down and flicked open the button on his jeans. Benji's mouth started salivating heavier. He gripped his thighs to keep his hands from reaching out and taking what he wanted.

"Good boy," Jay praised as he noticed Benji's restraint. "Do you want my cock, pet?"

Benji nodded, not trusting himself to speak. He licked his lips and swallowed. Jay unzipped his pants and shimmied them down his hips, showing off a pair of dark grey laced briefs. He leaned against the desk and stripped off his shirt. Benji took a moment to drink in the archivist. His pale ivory skin was covered with chest hair that trailed down his stomach towards his groin. His belly was soft and plump. Benji wanted to bury his head against it. His legs were gorgeous and his calves were toned from moving up and down library ladders daily. Jay cleared his throat and Benji met his eyes again.

"Come here, pet." Jay adjusted his dick beneath the lace. Benji rushed over as quickly as he could on his knees. It might not have been the most dignified movement, but he hoped he would get points for enthusiasm. When he settled back into his submissive position, Jay tilted his chin up again and smiled.

"Well done, Benj." Jay cupped his cheek and Benji leaned into the touch. Jay moved his thumb across his lips and when Benji's lips parted, Jay slid his thumb into Benji's warm mouth. Benji began sucking on the digit. He hoped he would do a good enough job with Jay's thumb that he would be rewarded with his cock. He flicked his tongue along the creases of Jay's knuckles and lightly teased the tip. He hollowed his cheeks and took the thumb to the bottom knuckle. Jay's hand lightly gripped the side of his jaw and squeezed. He slowly pulled his thumb out and put it in his own mouth, sucking it clean of Benji's saliva.

"You're impressive, pet," Jay acknowledged. "I think you've earned my cock. Don't you?"

Benji nodded again. Jay moved his hand behind Benji's head and eased him forward. Benji's face hit the lace and he breathed deeply. Jay smelled like a hint of leather and parchment as if the library was part of his DNA. Benji opened his mouth and sucked on Jay's dick through the lace. Jay let out a pleased hum and Benji teased him more enthusiastically.

Jay let him play for a little longer and then guided his head back.

"You're being a very eager and good boy, pet." Benji tingled with excitement when Jay called him "pet." It made him feel special and cherished. The praise Jay lavished on him pushed Benji closer and closer to the edge of euphoria.

Benji watched with increased anticipation as Jay pulled his briefs down and stepped back into his space. Benji lunged forward, eager to swallow Jay's hard, dripping cock and taste him fully, but Jay stopped him just before Benji could wrap his mouth around him.

"Patience, pet. I want you to take your time. Savor it. Enjoy the experience." Jay bent down and kissed Benji's forehead before leaning back on his desk and spreading his legs a little wider to give Benji better access.

Benji did as he was instructed. He liked being a good boy. He needed the praise that Jay gave him. He craved it as much as he craved breathing, as if it was part of his genetic makeup.

Slowly, he stuck his tongue out and lapped at the tip of Jay's cock that was dripping with precum. It was salty and addictive. Benji let himself get another taste before moving his mouth down the shaft toward Jay's balls. His lips nibbled at the vein on the underside of Jay's dick and Jay hissed with satisfaction.

"Good boy, that feels like heaven."

Benji stuck his tongue out and pressed the top of it along the vein. Jay's cock twitched and Jay gripped the edge of the desk.

Seeing Jay close to losing control made Benji work even harder. Benji took Jay deep in his throat and hollowed his cheeks. He pulled off and teased the head of Jay's cock. He sucked on Jay's balls and lapped at his taint. When Jay was panting and babbling praises, Benji knew he was almost there.

He looked up at Jay through watering eyes. "Fuck my throat. Please."

Jay unlocked his grip of the desk and gently placed his hands on either side of Benji's head, tangling them in his hair. And then he started moving. Thrust after thrust until his cum shot down Benji's throat. Jay began to pull out, but Benji moved with him and swallowed down every drop that Jay released. His body was singing, and Jay was right there with the praises to harmonize.

They stayed there for a moment while they both caught their breaths and then Benji noticed his knees throbbing. He was so focused on bringing Jay pleasure that he had been ignoring any signs his body was giving him.

Jay held out a hand and helped Benji up off the floor. He waited for Benji to stretch out his aching knees and then lead him over to the green velvet wingback armchair.

"Your throne, my king," Jay said.

"I'm upgraded from pet to king, now, am I?" Benji teased.

"It's all reverence. You are amazing no matter what part you're playing," Jay admitted.

Benji lowered himself down on the chair like the royalty Jay called him. A still naked Jay sat in his lap and Benji wrapped his arms around him.

"Will you let me take care of you now?" Jay whispered in Benji's ear. The small hairs on his jaw and neck stood on end.

"Please," Benji whispered back.

Jay slid off his lap and onto his knees. He reached to the front of Benji's pants and waited as Benji lifted his hips.

Jay unbuttoned them and slid them down off of Benji's wide hips.

Benji held his breath as Jay drank in what he saw. Benji knew that having a vagina rather than a natal penis was different, but he loved his boy pussy. He loved that he had two holes to play with, two holes that could be stuffed full and pounded. He just hoped Jay liked them, too.

Just as Benji was getting up the courage to break the silence, Jay lunged forward and kissed him, straddling his lap again. His hands made their way down Benji's still clothed torso and cupped his labia. His middle finger slipped between the folds into the wetness. Benji gasped and began to grind his hips against Jay's hand. A second finger found its way in and Jay began exploring Benji's pussy. He ground the palm of his hand against Benji's clit and Benji started moving faster. Jay's fingers started stroking and teasing Benji's hole causing him to become wetter.

"You're such a good boy, Benji. Look at you being all wet for me. You ride my hand so well, maybe I should let you ride my face. Would you like that, my king?" Jay's sultry and dominant tone was back. The thought of Jay's mouth anywhere near Benji's holes made him shudder with delight.

"Yes, please. Let me ride your face."

Jay helped Benji off the chair and they maneuvered over to one of chaise longes. Before they lowered themselves into position, Jay tugged at Benji's shirt. He lifted it off to reveal his binder. Benji removed that next letting his tits become unbound from the magic that flattened them in place. His hairy chest and breasts made him feel powerful. He loved that his body was uniquely his.

Jay reached out and caressed Benji's sides, moving his hands up slowly toward his breasts. When he cupped them both and started playing with Benji's nipples, Benji tipped his head back. Benji felt Jay's mouth start sucking on his nipple and moaned. He was already teetering on the edge of coming and didn't want to miss out on riding Jay's face like he'd been promised.

He pushed the top of Jay's head, directing him down and then reclined on the lounge spreading himself out like the feast he wanted to be. Jay devoured him with his eyes, drinking in every inch of him, from his plump belly to his thick thighs with the single dark freckle on the left side of his hip. Jay reverently bowed next to Benji and kissed him, slowly moving down his body, playing with the thick hair on his breasts and belly as he went. Benji felt himself leaking and was glad he had that cleaning spell down. The thought of leaving a stain on the chaise had him starting to blush, or maybe that was Jay's mouth that was teasing his inner thighs. Benji squirmed trying to position his pelvis closer to Jay's hot mouth. Jay placed his arm against Benji's stomach, holding him in place with more strength than Benji was expecting.

He didn't have long to dwell on Jay's unexpected strength, however, because Jay's tongue licked Benji's pussy from his vagina to his clit, and then his whole mouth followed.

"Jay," Benji cried out. He hoped there was a silencing charm on the door because he'd hate to be interrupted now that Jay was tasting him.

Jay sucked on Benji's clit and brought his two fingers back to continue their earlier exploration. They teased the opening of his vagina and Benji felt the tensing of his muscles beginning when both fingers entered him. Jay still had his mouth on Benji's clit, and Benji was beginning to feel the tingle of an orgasm forming again.

"J-Jay. Ahhh. So good. Wanna-wanna fuck your face,"

Benji panted as he tried controlling his orgasm, keeping it from tipping over the top. He closed his eyes, straining to stay in control. The pressure from Jay's mouth disappeared as he pulled off suddenly and Benji stayed where he reclined, panting to catch his breath. When he finally opened his eyes, Jay was standing above him, lust-drunk and ruffled from where Benji had been fisting his curls.

Jay held out his hand and helped Benji up off the chaise. He kissed him deeply, licking into his mouth so that Benji tasted his own wetness on Jay's tongue.

"A promise is a promise," Jay said, lowering himself down and summoning a pillow to support his neck.

Benji took a deep breath and then straddled Jay's chest. Jay gave him one last hungry look before positioning himself further between Benji's thighs. Benji felt the warmth of Jay's tongue start to tease his holes again as Jay's hands cupped his ass. He gripped the arm of the chaise and rocked his body, chasing the pleasure that Jay's mouth was providing.

He found his rhythm and then increased his speed until his eyesight began to tunnel and all he could focus on was the building sensation. Faster and faster, Benji rode Jay's face until he tipped over the edge and came. His clit became too sensitive, and he scooted back so he was kneeling on either side of Jay's chest, keeping his body hovering over the archivist.

Jay looked up at Benji, his chin and mouth wet. It took a few minutes for Jay's eyes to fully come back into focus. They both stayed there panting, Benji continuing to grip the arm of the chaise and Jay moving his hands along Benji's outer thighs in soothing movements. Neither man spoke in the moment, they just basked in the pleasure they were able to coax from each other.

chapter twelve

JAY HADN'T FELT this boneless in years. If he hadn't been physically touching Benji, he might have thought he'd ascended to a different plane. After a few moments, Benji shifted and Jay reluctantly let go of his thighs to let him climb off his chest. Jay held out his arm and Benji snuggled in next to him on the chaise.

"That was..." Benji started, still catching his breath.

Stunning. Amazing. Mind-Blowing. Jay thought of a countless number of descriptors for what they had done, but none of them would do it proper justice.

"Perfect," he settled on.

"Exactly." Jay felt Benji smile against his shoulder.

They lay there, naked, until their cum became uncomfortable. Benji helped Jay up off the chaise and muttered a cleaning spell while Jay walked around the room to grab their clothing. He handed Benji his clothes and watched as the professor began to dress. Jay hoped that wouldn't be the last time he was able to enjoy the man's glorious body. He could easily find himself addicted to the sounds Benji made when Jay found his pleasure points. He was feeling more rejuvenated in the moment than he normally would be after spending a night sleeping at his desk.

When both men had finished putting themselves back together and any hints of impropriety were cleaned up, Jay led Benji back towards the desk.

"That was one hell of a prize, Professor," Jay laughed as he started reorganizing the tomes and papers he had magicked away.

"You're telling me," Benji chuckled back. Both men looked at each other and then broke into a fit of giggles. Jay hadn't found anyone to laugh with like this since his undergrad days. Everything in the archive seemed to brighten with their joy as their auras mixed and expanded out from them.

"Please tell me that won't be the last time we do that," Benji urged.

"Oh gods, no." Jay kissed the tip of Benji's nose. "We can do that anytime you want. Maybe not in here, though. I don't think I'll be able to look at my chaise without getting hard. I can't imagine if the entire archive turned into one giant reminder of the fun we can have together."

Benji beamed and Jay was glad that they were in agreement. Knowing that he would get more chances to worship the professor's body settled something in Jay's soul. He watched as their auras, still bright and pulsing from their orgasms, began to sync their rhythmic beat like Benji's heartbeat was matching Jay's. It was a sensation Jay had never experienced before, but he felt powerful being so connected with someone. He took Benji's hand and felt a spark tingle up his arm as their auras brightened at the spot where their hands connected.

"So can I maybe take you to dinner sometime?" Benji asked tentatively.

"You'll have to." Jay nudged him in the side. "I won the bet."

"You found it?" Benji leaned over the documents that had reorganized themselves on the desk.

Jay flipped the page on a small tome to expose a handwritten journal entry from legendary explorer Edwina Bogwin, one of the architects who would make way for modern day magical practices. Her exploits were renowned throughout the magical world. She had found a way to set up a permanently portable teleportation sigil to bring on her explorations, and Jay seemed to have one of her actual diaries.

"How did you get this?" Benji asked, shocked to see the 800–year old tome in near pristine condition.

"Would you believe it was in a box in a box in a trunk somewhere over there?" Jay pointed towards the back of the stacks.

"Strangely, yes, I would. Your predecessor was not the most organized." Benji shuddered at a memory. "You've brought this place a long way."

Jay smiled at the praise of his accomplishments. When he had taken over from the last archivist, Scarpial B had been in a state of chaos. There was no cataloguing system that would make sense to anyone but the archivist in charge, and while Jay could acknowledge that each archivist had their own spin on organization, there were some universal practices that were seen as standard. He had been taught to use the Universal Standard as the basis for his own catalogue and then build from there.

"The first thing I did when I got here was get organized. It took nearly my whole first month to get things back to Universal Standard," Jay admitted. "I was beyond thrilled to find this diary. It seems to be centered around one of her later exploits, and I had only skimmed through it before setting it aside, but I remember she talks about working with a few other magical specialists to traverse this cavern system. When you were talking about the work you did with that collective of other professors to create the safe path through the forest, I was reminded of this book and one of the passages I read, where she talked about the conditions of the cavern. In that particular passage, she mentions seeing a faint blue glow at the bottom of one of the cavern pools. The team worked to create a crude breathing device so they could go check it out."

Jay pointed to a particular excerpt and Benji leaned over closer to read it aloud.

"We discovered the dying remnant of an element long thought expired from this world. The glow contained within was that of the cobalt ichor under crystallized lava born under a sunless water. It was nothing like I had ever seen in my life. While some in our party wished to exhume the piece for further study, we overall made the decision to leave it in place under the hopes it might continue to grow, as we do not know the nature of how such an element is borne."

Jay watched as the wheels in Benji's head started going into overdrive. His aura was excitedly lashing out in little bursts of light like spurts of flame from a campfire.

"Okay, okay. So, this means I've got some experimenting to do."

"Wait," Jay stopped Benji with a touch to his arm. "There's more. She goes on to describe more of the cave, including properties in some of the water they brought back to test at their base camp."

Benji slid his hand to Jay's waist and turned the archivist to face him. Jay gasped at the intense affection in Benji's gaze. Benji swallowed his gasp with a kiss. As much as Jay had enjoyed the dominant role in their earlier foray, he melted under Benji's touch now, feeling pliant and ready to submit to whatever Benji wanted to do. He enthusiastically welcomed Benji's hands as they roved over his body and eagerly met the professor's tongue with his own as Benji deepened the kiss.

After what felt like eternity and no time at all, Jay pulled away to catch his breath. He looked over at Benji's mussed hair and disheveled appearance and smiled. This man would be his undoing in the best way. Despite the pull to return to kissing Benji's slightly swollen lips, and possibly repeat what they had done earlier, Jay knew they needed to stay focused on the project.

"You're a distraction," Benji said with a heavy tone of teasing lacing his words.

"I was just thinking the same thing about you, Professor." Jay smirked.

They stood there for a long moment, lost in each other's eyes, until Benji cleared his throat.

"So, I have a theory, but I'm going to need to take some notes from the book to make sure I have all the information I'll need." He looked around for his satchel which contained his many notebooks and papers.

Jay cleared off a space for him to work and then muttered an incantation to start the tea kettle he used when doing his research.

The two men settled into a flow, with Benji reading Edwina Bogwin's journal and stopping to take notes, while Jay pulled additional references from the archives they could use to cross reference details. By the time the first sun was setting, Benji had calculations and a firm plan, while Jay had a whole cart of materials to reshelve.

Tomorrow, he thought. He was exhausted, but happy from one of the best days he'd experienced since starting this job at Vhakyllus University.

"So… when can I take you out on that date?" Benji asked as the men began their trek down the spiral staircase to the library's exit.

"I'd say tonight, but I'm exhausted from today, and I want to make sure I'm good company for whatever we do. Tomorrow, maybe?" Jay offered.

"Tomorrow is perfect. I'll pick you up here at three?"

"Perfect," Jay echoed.

After a quick, heated kiss, Benji squeezed Jay's hand and walked away toward the Transmutation corridor and his office. Jay began to walk the other way to the school's portal site, so he could head home and try to rest in anticipation of the next day's date.

chapter thirteen

FROM THE MOMENT he woke up, Benji's mind was on the date he had planned for that evening. Every spare opportunity he had was spent going over his idea. From everything he had learned about Jay so far, Benji was certain that the quiet beauty of their excursion was the right choice. When it finally came time to meet, Benji looked himself over in the mirror on the back of his office door, straightened his clothes with the help of some basic magic, and began to walk briskly toward the library.

Jay was standing at the reference desk in the library's entry foyer talking to Felix. Benji watched for a moment as Jay's heterochromatic eyes lit up with laughter. Benji wished he was able to see Jay's aura the same way other aurals could. He wanted to see the dance of colors he was certain were twirling around him now. He longed to know what it was like when their auras mixed. Jay had tried describing it to him once, and as much of an artist as he was, he wasn't certain he grasped the full picture. Part of what intrigued him so much about Alchvhybium was that it moved in a way that was unlike anything else he could see. It's how he imagined auras moving—flowing and pulsing with the energy of their human. Jay turned and noticed him. Jay's smile beamed so brightly, and Benji thought he could almost see a brief glimpse of Jay's aura, but it was gone when he blinked, so Benji chalked it up to his imagination. He strode over to greet Jay hoping words would come to him by the time he had traversed the small distance.

They didn't.

"Hi," he squeaked, internally facepalming from the lack of a better greeting. Benji never got nervous around people, even when he had met his idol, Bethany Storriel, so what was it about Jay that made him tongue-tied and twitterpated?

Jay said his goodbyes to Felix and reached out to take Benji's hand in his as the two walked off to the University's portal station.

They joined the queue of students and other University staff and faculty who were waiting their turn to leave for the day. Benji looked around the grand hall with its mahogany and stained-glass details.

"Do you not take the portals regularly?" Jay asked, noticing Benji's gaze on an intricately detailed stained-glass panel depicting one of the Myths of Arbose.

"No, usually I'll only portal if the weather is terrible or if I'm running extremely late. Or if it's urgent," he tacked on. "Usually, I walk. I live just on the other side of the forest. The commute isn't long and I enjoy the time I get to spend outside, since I'm usually indoors all day."

Jay squeezed his hand. "You'll have to show me sometime. I wish I could have found something close like that."

"Where are you staying?"

"Outer Bedfordshire, still."

Benji was surprised that Jay was still living near his

Alma Mater, Olde Bedfordshire University of Magical Arts.

"That's a long commute, or it would be." By non-magical transportation, it was a good three-hour drive or hour-long train ride once you accounted for all the stops.

Jay hummed his agreement. "Thankfully, since I'm still near OBUOMA, I'm able to use their teleportation hub. It was one of the contingencies I asked for when I started since coming in mid-year meant I wouldn't have time to really search for a new place to live."

"I'm glad they were able to work that out for you."

Benji wanted to continue the intimate conversations they normally had but students were all around them, some even peering at where their hands were connected and whispering together. Benji knew he had a reputation as one of the cooler professors in the school, at least in the Transmutation and Alchemy departments, but that didn't mean he enjoyed being the center of gossip, especially when he could see it happening right in front of him. Despite the discomfort he began to feel, he didn't let go of Jay's hand.

Jay was playing with something in his pocket and looked a little jittery and uncertain, much like a startled Taaques, so Benji steeled himself to take Jay's mind away from whatever was making him anxious.

"Any guesses on where we're going?" he asked. Jay dropped whatever was in his pocket and focused his attention back on Benji. He visibly relaxed as a pulsing vibration reached out to Benji. "What was that?" he asked, startled.

"What was what?" Jay questioned.

"That vibration." He leaned in to whisper in Jay's ear. "Is it something in your pocket or are you just excited to see me?"

Jay laughed and Benji scrunched up his face at the unexpected loudness.

"Sorry," Jay apologized, still laughing. "That was the worst thing anyone has ever said. It's such an outdated pickup line." Then he leaned into Benji's ear and whispered, "and you don't need to use one because you've already got me."

A pleasant shiver went down Benji's spine and butterflies flipped in his stomach. *Oh, this man.*

"But in all seriousness, I don't know what vibration you're talking about," Jay admitted.

"Weird." Benji thought about it for a minute. "It felt like a cat's purr that bumped up against me when you focused your attention on me. Maybe I was imagining it."

"No, I don't think you were. Magic is still revealing itself to us every day—whether it's lost magics returning or new iterations and evolutions of existing magic, society is forever discovering new parts of this universe. So sure, maybe whatever you felt was a fluke, but let me know if you feel it again."

"I will," Benji assured him. He could see the research side of the archivist peeking out, desperate to take over, so Benji squeezed Jay's hand. "I promise."

"Thank you."

It was finally their turn to take the teleport and Benji handed a piece of paper with their itinerary and destination over to the clerk who kept record of every trip made through the university's sigils.

"Will you tell me where we're headed?" Jay asked as they stepped up to one of the circles.

"South Lakeshore Aquarium," Benji said and stepped onto the sigil. Jay hurriedly followed him and they waited as the familiar sensation of being transported from one space to another overtook them.

They landed and both men took some time to settle. Jay handed Benji a ginger chew from his pocket as they walked to the recovery area.

"Try this. It helps. My friend Milly and her coven make them in Belherston. It'll help settle your stomach and take away any lingering effects."

Gods, I love magic, Benji thought as he popped the candy in his mouth.

"Thank you."

Benji retook Jay's hand, and pulled him into a hug, but began to feel the purring sensation again.

"Don't move, Jay, but I feel that vibration again. It's resonating at my chest currently." Benji tried to make note of any small detail he could, but he kept getting the sense that Jay was like a cat, purring on his chest.

"I still can't feel it, but I think something is happening because our aura mixing is swirling and dancing in a way I've never experienced before."

Jay held his hand to Benji's face and Benji felt the vibrations getting stronger where Jay touched him.

"I think I might be feeling our auras reacting to each other."

"What makes you say that?" Jay asked with a whisper.

"Because when you moved your hand close to my face, the vibrations got stronger where you touched me. Did the aura reaction intensify?"

"It did." Jay looked at Benji in disbelief and awe. "Benji, I think you can feel auras."

Benji laughed. He had just said that, but Jay seemed to be taking a longer time to process it. His laughter turned to giggles, which in turn made Jay start laughing. They both doubled over with hysterics feeding off each other like a closed-loop system.

"Come on, let's go get something to eat," Benji said,

taking Jay's hand in his after they finally got their laughter under control.

It was a short walk to the Alley's End tea shop, a small restaurant that offered a tea service and tasty treats according to the website Benji had found earlier. He looked up at the clock in the center of the square and was relieved to see they still had plenty of time to make it before their reservation. The walk took them across the cobblestone square and down an alley lit by fairy lights gently bobbing like they were floating on water instead of air.

Benji almost bumped into Jay when they exited the narrow alley into a garden with a clear magical roof to keep out any adverse weather, while allowing patrons to watch the sky. It was bordered by hedges and each table was surrounded by camellia shrubs to give them privacy. It was more romantic and beautiful than Benji could have ever imagined.

"Hi, do you have a reservation or were you just looking for a dark corner down the end of the alley?" The hostess greeted them cheekily.

"We have a reservation. It's, uh, under Rollins," Benji said, full of charm, while Jay stayed still with his mouth agape. Benji started to worry he may have overdone it with his choice of restaurant.

"Right this way," she said and led them to a table surrounded by a wall of eight-foot-tall shrubs with light pink and yellow flowers blooming along it. They sat on mismatched chairs that coordinated well but clearly didn't originate from the same collection. The entire space was decorated with an eclectic style of curated designs tied together with a dark-red-and-gold color scheme. The hostess left them with some menus and the two men settled into comfortable padded armchairs.

Jay still didn't say anything.

"Is this too much?" Benji asked.

Jay shook his head and took Benji's hand over the table. The vibration he felt at the touch pulsed like a heartbeat rather than a purr.

"It's amazing. Truly Benji, I don't think I could have imagined a more perfect first date spot if I had a thousand years."

Benji glowed with pride and the vibration intensified. He let himself enjoy the feeling of their connection and then pulled his hand back when it settled down.

"I don't know if I'm ever going to get used to that," he admitted.

"The vibration again?" Jay asked.

"Yeah, a different pattern this time. Like a beating heart."

"The visual pattern was different this time, too. I think we have a valid theory here, Professor."

"You're the research expert," Benji said with a smile.

"Oh, we'll definitely need to do more… research," Jay's voice turned sultry and suggestive.

Benji looked around and confirmed they were still alone before getting out of his chair and kneeling in front of Jay. He pulled him down and brought their mouths together for a deep and messy kiss. He kept it brief but passionate. The vibrations reverberated through Benji's whole body, making his hair stand on end. He almost caved and cancelled the rest of the evening so they could go somewhere private and explore their new connection, but he forced himself to pull away from Jay's electric lips. He sat back on his chair and picked up his menu to keep his hands from reaching for Jay again.

"What was that for?" Jay asked, looking a little drunk from the kiss.

"Would you believe me if I said I was just testing a theory?"

"Just?"

"No, not just. I really wanted to kiss you again."

"Well, you can do that any time you want, *pet*."

A shiver ran down Benji's spine and he clenched the menu harder to keep himself from getting back down on his knees to worship Jay's body right there in the middle of the restaurant.

Just then, their server came into the clearing and both men looked over at him. Jay pulled a small stone from his pocket and was fidgeting with it while they listened to the server listing off that day's specials.

They ordered and Benji hoped he chose well. He wasn't usually a tea drinker, so he hoped the menu was accurate when listing the tasting notes.

They waited for their tea and meals to come and made small talk about different observations about campus. Both men were trying to avoid touching each other. The privacy their space granted was too tempting with the new discovery about the vibrations. Benji wished he could figure out a way for Jay to experience even a small amount of the sensation.

"It's really difficult trying not to touch you right now," he admitted.

"Just think of how satisfying it will be when we finally get the chance," Jay offered.

"The man is dominant one time and now he thinks he can control my orgasms," Benji joked.

"Touching me is orgasmic?"

Benji just winked and bit his bottom lip in a way he hoped was seductive. It wasn't. Jay burst out laughing. Benji joined in right along with him.

"Touching you is unlike anything I've ever experienced. And, full disclosure, I don't mind you edging me."

"Noted," Jay acknowledged, wiping the tears of laughter from his eyes.

The tea and dinner came, and the server poured their first cups and instructed them on how to use the self-filling kettle. When they were alone again, Benji watched as Jay took his first sips of the tea he chose and practically melted back into the chair with sigh of satisfaction and peace.

"That good, huh?" he asked.

"This is my favorite tea. I'm so happy they have it. It's a bit niche, so I wasn't expecting them to have it. Here, try some." Jay handed his porcelain teacup to Benji who took a sip of the tea. He was surprised to enjoy it. It was sweeter than he expected and smooth. There was no bitterness that he usually experienced whenever he'd tried steeping his own in the past.

"Wow, that's delicious." Benji admitted. He handed Jay's teacup back to him before he would be tempted to drink the whole thing.

"It gets better the more steeps you do. I usually get about 4 or 5 from the same leaves when I make it at home."

"Wow, that's a bit more economical than my regular Jack's runs."

Jay smiled. "What do you think of yours?"

"I'm a little nervous to try."

"You picked a pretty safe option. It's a blend rather than a single-origin option, so you're more likely to find something in it you like."

"The menu said it tasted chocolatey, and I'm a big fan of chocolate." Benji picked up his own cup and sniffed it, surprised that the aroma wasn't as strong as he would expect. He took a tentative sip, swished the tea around in his mouth, and swallowed.

"It's good, but I don't know. It's just not quite there."

"Try adding a little milk or cream," Jay suggested.

Benji doctored up his cup and tried again. This time, he enjoyed the taste much more. The richness of the chocolate came through with hints of vanilla and earthiness.

"You're right," Benji admitted. "That does help. It's delicious. Though, I think I still prefer the one you got."

"I'll share it with you."

Jay poured some of his tea into Benji's empty cup and then started the kettle to begin steeping another pot.

By the time they left, they had drunk four steepings of Jay's favorite tea, enjoyed a whole tray of sandwiches, and a smaller platter of varied desserts.

They slowly walked up the alley back toward the main square. Right before they stepped out into the open area, Jay stopped and pressed Benji against the wall with one hand pinned against his chest. He stepped into his space, one leg placed between Benji's, and leaned in close to Benji's ear.

"Thank you, Benj. That was the best first date I've ever had. I can't wait for the next one."

And then Jay kissed him. Benji submitted to Jay's dominance, the vibration and passion making him wet with desire. When Jay finally broke off the kiss, Benji had to catch his breath, grateful he was leaning against the sturdy wall as he was pretty sure he would have fallen over if left to his own devices.

Gathering his wits, he put his hands on Jay's waist and brought him in close.

"The night's not over, Jay. We still have more adventure

to enjoy." And then Benji kissed the tip of Jay's nose before pulling them both out into the open square.

chapter fourteen

JAY HAD ALWAYS WANTED to visit the aquarium. With as much time as he spent reading about different creatures that lived throughout the world, he never really got the chance to experience them, even in controlled settings. The closest he got was watching nature documentaries in between study sessions during undergrad.

He followed as Benji led them through the doors and presented both of their tickets to the employee working the admission desk. They were both handed badges on lanyards. Jay slipped his over his head and marveled at the picture of an octojel, one of his favorite marine creatures, depicted with a lenticular lens to make it appear to be floating through the ocean's depths. Jay lightly scraped his fingernails over the raised surface of the badge and delighted in the tactile feeling. He hoped they wouldn't need to return the badges at the end of the night because it would be the perfect keepsake from his and Benji's first date.

He watched as Benji's aura swirled around him, the sunshine hue morphing into the colors of a late afternoon sun right before a sunset hit—more golden, bordering on orange, than the dandelion yellow he was used to. Jay really wanted to study the correlation between their auras mixing and the new vibration patterns Benji was feeling, but he didn't want research and work to encroach on their date any more than it already had.

Jay had learned to compartmentalize as part of his research methods. He found that his brain would take him off on tangents and down rabbit holes if he didn't. Part of being a good archivist and researcher was staying on task, so he employed those same methods now and put aside his aural curiosity to focus on his marine-life curiosity.

He reached out and took Benji's hand again, smiling as their auras blended together into the familiar green that Jay found ever-increasing comfort in. Benji led him through a crowd of families congregating around a recreation of a blue whale and its baby that were floating above everyone and started to walk up the walkway around the exterior of the lobby.

The walkway was a ramp that wove around all six walls and had hallways branching off for different exhibits. The aquarium was part museum and part conservatory. Most of the inhabitants were there because they either couldn't be released into the wild or they were there as part of a rehabilitation effort. Jay couldn't quite tell where Benji was taking him, but he was so gobsmacked by the surprise of Benji's restaurant choice earlier, he followed quietly behind, excited to see where this adventure would take them.

Benji kept going up the walkway until they passed the top of the whale re-creations and made it to the fourth floor. Jay tried not to let his excitement take over as they walked down the bioluminescence corridor. Bioluminescent creatures had always been his favorite. It was like they had an aura everyone could see. Their glow gave him comfort, and it was always blue, like his. When he was little, he thought that they were all magical creatures because of their glow. Some of them, like the octojel, were magic, but others were a result of science and nature. Jay often attributed his fascination around bioluminescent creatures as the catalyst to his ambition to become an archivist and researcher. He briefly considered going into marine biology, but then he realized he was much more fascinated by learning rather than being hands-on.

He also realized in that moment that he had never expressed any of these early childhood desires to Benji. So how did he know to bring Jay here? Out of all the exhibits in the aquarium, Benji had beelined for the one that Jay was most excited to explore.

"Hey Benji?" Jay asked.

"Yeah?" Benji turned to look at him, slowing their pace but still continuing on to the exhibit.

"How did you know that I'd want to come here?"

"To the aquarium? I wasn't completely certain, but the tea set next to your desk featured an octojel, so I figured you'd probably enjoy it."

He paid attention. He noticed and remembered things. It shouldn't be such a startling revelation, but Jay hadn't met many people who remembered things about him *for* him. Usually, they just remembered things about him that they found useful. This was different and the realization made his aura surge and brighten the dark corridor. He got a few looks from other aurals in the vicinity, but he couldn't help it. Benji made him feel special. He worked to suppress his aura so it would be less distracting. That was another thing he got good at doing over the years. Elder aurals assumed that outbursts meant you couldn't control yourself and were too excitable. He tamped down the memory of many scoldings he had received during training as a youth and focused back on Benji, who was staring at him with a curious expression.

"What's going on in your head? Did I pick wrong? Oh shit, are you afraid of octojel and the tea set is a gag gift or a type of exposure therapy?" Benji started rambling.

"No, no. That's not it at all," Jay assured his professor. "Octojel are my favorite. You picked correctly. I was just remembering something from my youth about aural training, and it threw me off for a second. I'm good now. Promise."

Benji seemed to believe him and they walked around the corner into the bioluminescence room. It was shaped like a circle with glass walls taking up about 80-percent of the space. In the middle of the room was a shallow tank that showed some bioluminescent sand and allowed small children or curious guests to interact directly.

"Is this what you see when you see someone's aura?" Benji asked, poking his finger into the sand and watching as it glowed brighter where he touched it.

"A bit. Honestly, that's why octojel are my favorite creatures and I'm so fascinated by bioluminescence. When I was a kid, I thought I could see their aura, too because they glowed. It wasn't exactly the case, but it still put me on the track to be where I am today."

"That's amazing. Thank you for sharing that with me." Benji seemed genuinely interested to learn more about Jay's lore, and it surprised him again. He needed to recalibrate his expectations of other people if he was going to spend more time around those that actually cared about truly getting to know him.

Something caught Jay's eye and he turned to see it—an octojel. He darted away from Benji, leaving him standing with his finger still in the sand, and rushed over to the glass where the glorious creature floated lazily by. It was the magical kin of an octopus with a number of tentacles that helped propel it along the sand and a defense mechanism that let it hide its bioluminescent nature through camouflage, but it also had characteristics of its jellyfish cousin in that it had a bulbous head and was able to let its tentacles go flaccid and flatten into a wavy appendage, allowing it to float along like a jellyfish. It was a way to lure unsuspecting prey into thinking it was a normal bioluminescent jellyfish and an easy target. But as soon as they got close, it would switch into octopus mode and attack. Jay had never seen it in person, but he regularly read accounts and watched animated simulations of what others had seen.

Seeing the creature float along right before his eyes was breathtaking. He was so entranced by its fluidity and grace, that he missed Benji's approach. Benji placed his hand around Jay's waist and Jay leaned into the touch.

"It's beautiful," Benji whispered as if not to break Jay's trance.

They stood there watching the octojel float around the tank, leaning on each other. Jay heard Benji's breath catch as a subluceo shark passed by the octojel, but both creatures avoided each other.

"Don't worry, it's not one of the octojel's predators. Or prey," Jay reassured him.

"Can you tell me more about it?"

Jay knew that Benji could easily read one of the plaques around the room that contained information about the creatures in the tank, but he was happy that Benji wanted to hear from him about his favorite creature.

"So, octojel use a bait and switch technique when they're hunting. They appear helpless and vulnerable to a jellyfish's predator, but as soon as something comes in for the kill, the octojel activates its tentacles and generally strangles the creature that tried to attack them. They've been known to also spin some creatures to disorient them and then strangle them. Usually, they only do that when the creature is much larger. But subluceo sharks are pretty much the puppies of the shark world. They eat, sure, but they're usually going after schools of smaller fish, not anything like a jellyfish or octojel." Jay's excitement started to grow, and with it, his aura, but he wasn't going to let anyone shame him for his joy. "They've had to adapt over the years and now they float amongst other jellyfish or as part of a pod of other octojel if they're trying to take down larger predators. Many predators will avoid them if they're floating solo like this one."

Benji hung on Jay's words, looking between him and the octojel.

"So what does it eat in this kind of setting? I can't imagine they'd put a bunch of predators in the tank."

"No, from what I've researched, they do similar enrichment activities like for octopi," Jay explained. "They'll bring in different containers and vessels that have food in them, but they'll lock it up and make the octojel work at getting it out. I've even heard about some aquariums and conservatories bringing in magical consultants to create additional obstacles that simulate some of the scenarios they'd experience in the wild."

"If you ever need a career change, I can imagine you'd be really good at something like that."

"Maybe when I retire," Jay joked.

They watched as the octojel floated behind some coral and out of sight, then they took in some of the other creatures in the room and Benji got a kick out of the subluceo shark playing what could only be described as a game of tag with some of the larger lizardfish. Eventually, they moved out of the bioluminescent corridor and back to the main atrium.

"Now I've got to know. What creature do you want to see?" Jay asked.

"Algaefish and cat's tail reeds," Benji responded without hesitation.

"To the river," Jay exclaimed and took the lead back down the ramp to the first floor. They skirted past a group of school kids gathering to leave and went outside to the river exhibit. It was just about dusk, and Jay picked up his pace so they could see the algaefish before it got too dark.

Benji squatted down near the river's edge as close as he could get and observed the surface-dwelling creatures. Jay had read about algaefish in his studies, but he was happy to listen to Benji talk about what he liked about the filter fish.

"I wish they had a rootent tree so I could see these guys in action. I've always been fascinated by the codependency that they have with each other. The rootent trees give the algaefish shelter and a bit of protection, while the algaefish keep the rootents free from mold and scum. Oh, look at that one," Benji exclaimed, pointing at a large flat algaefish with a large lily pad on its back. "Did you know that the lily pads are part of their feeding system and show the age of the fish? This one must be ancient."

Jay did know that algaefish relied on photosynthesis for the majority of their nutrition, but he didn't want to quiet Benji's chatter, so he listened as Benji continued to ramble. Jay enjoyed his rambling. He helped Benji up out of his squat and they walked over to look at the cat's tail reeds. A sign in front of the reeds talked about the cross-breeding efforts the conservation program was doing to help preserve an endangered variety of cat's tail, the Torbie. Benji and Jay read that the aquarium had planted tortoiseshell and tabby varieties and let them cross pollinate resulting in the Torbie patterned tails.

"Why cat's tails?" Jay asked.

"I love cats," Benji explained. "I wasn't able to have one growing up, but we lived near a creek that had orange tabby cat's tails growing along the edge. I used to go down and sit among them while I played in the mud and watched the algaefish. If they get used to you and like you, they'll flick around like an actual cat. It wasn't quite the same, but it was a good alternative."

"Do you have a cat now?"

"Not officially." Jay waited for Benji to continue. "There's a neighborhood cat that I feed and let in my apartment during the night, so she has a place to stay safe. We have a nice bond and she listens to me talk about my day. It's nice."

"Sounds almost like having your own unofficial familiar."

"Honestly, sometimes it feels that way," Benji admitted. "But then she's usually gone whenever I wake up. She knows when I need her though."

"That's fantastic. I'd love to meet her sometime." Jay hoped he wasn't being too forward.

"Oh, I'm sure you will." Benji winked at him.

They sat on a bench and watched the cat's tails sway in the breeze and enjoyed the second sun's setting. Jay leaned into Benji's side, breathing in the fresh air and faint smell of paper pulp on his jacket. After a moment, Jay felt a nudge.

"Jay, gorgeous, wake up. It's probably time to get you home." Jay opened his eyes to see the sun had fully set and the path along the creek and back into the aquarium was lined with lights similar to those leading down to the tea house. He yawned and stretched his limbs.

"You're probably right. It's been a long day—a long week, really," Jay admitted. He let Benji help him up. They fell into step and headed back out through the atrium and into the square. They joined a queue of other people in the teleportation terminal, but the line moved faster than it did at the university.

When they made it back through the portal, Benji walked Jay back to the entrance of the library.

"Thank you for a fantastic afternoon and evening. This was the best first date I've ever been on," Jay acknowledged. He kissed Benji on the cheek.

Benji wrapped his arms around Jay. "It was fantastic, wasn't it? I'm glad you had a good time. I can't wait to go on more adventures with you."

Their auras kicked up activity and Jay noticed Benji's eyes got wide with the intensity.

"We've got to figure out this vibration thing," Jay mused. "It's going to drive me wild if we don't."

"As much as I like you a bit wild, I don't want to do anything that will tax your mind," Benji responded.

"Why thank you, good sir," Jay joked. "How about this. We both have theories about it. Let's see who can figure it out first."

"And what does the winner get?"

Jay bit his lip and looked around. No one was in the hall or anywhere within hearing distance.

"The winner, Professor Rollins, gets to choose who tops first."

Benji let out a little whimper before steeling his gaze. "You're on."

They sealed the agreement with a kiss.

Jay pulled away to go back to his office and grab the items he had left behind so he could go home. "You're on, Professor." He cackled as he walked into the library, Benji watching him as he went.

chapter fifteen

OVER THE NEXT WEEK, Benji was riding high from his date with Jay. He went to class in the mornings and then worked on grading and coursework in the afternoons. Usually he would find himself heading to the library after a pit stop at Jack's to bring Jay a beverage and a treat.

He enjoyed the new intimacies they were able to share. They shared kisses regularly, but nothing like what had happened in the library that first day. Both men were spurred on by the promise of the bet's rewards that they kept their encounters mostly chaste. That is, until one day when Benji came back to his office after class to find Jay sitting in his chair wearing a corduroy suit with elbow patches and a turtleneck that made him look like a present waiting to be unwrapped. Benji shut his door and locked it behind him, tossing a silencing charm around the perimeter.

"Well well, what do we have here?" he practically growled as Jay looked up from the book he was reading. Benji was vibrating with anticipation.

"Oh hey, Benji," Jay casually said, not acknowledging

the hungry look in the professor's eyes. "Just wanted to pop in after my conference and see how you're doing."

That's right, Jay had been asked to present at a one-day conference for archivists about his glasses and cataloguing system. The sight of the delectable man had thrown everything else out of his brain. *Gods he was horny.* Benji tried to tamp down his desires and focus on listening to the man who was making him all hot and bothered. He tried. Or at least that would be what he'd tell anyone who asked.

Benji strode over to Jay and drew him up from the chair, pulling him into an embrace that quickly turned into a passionate kiss. Both men were clutching at each other like they hadn't seen each other in years rather than a day. Benji brushed his tongue against Jay's mouth and when Jay opened for him, he pressed inside, tasting the familiar chocolate, vanilla, and earthy flavors that lingered after Jay had his daily treat from Jack's. Jay's tongue swirled around Benji's, and the two men played with each other, exchanging teasing nips and chasing their tongues in and out of each other's mouths. Benji couldn't wait to be inside Jay for real or to have Jay inside him. He didn't actually have a preference, he was just excited to connect.

Benji moved his hands underneath Jay's cotton turtleneck to feel his smooth skin, covered in light hair. He moved from worshipping Jay's mouth to lavishing praises along his jawline and neck. Benji breathed in the scent of Jay's cologne—leather and tea with a hint of bergamot. It turned him on even more and he snaked one of his hands up Jay's chest to tweak his nipple. He could feel Jay's hard cock poking at him beneath his suit pants. Benji wanted to worship that cock. He nibbled at Jay's earlobe and then sunk to his knees, undoing Jay's belt and the button and zipper on his pants. With one hand, he tugged the pants down and with the other he pushed Jay's hips back so that the man was sitting on the edge of Benji's office chair.

Benji didn't hesitate but instead swallowed Jay down to the base. Benji again breathed in Jay's scent, but instead of the cologne, this was his natural scent. Benji began to hollow his cheeks and suck with a fervor. The hand that had pushed Jay's hips back onto the chair found its way up to his nipples again and Benji was delighted to find they were hard. When he squeezed one, Jay gave out a moan that went all the way through Benji. He was already wet and wanted friction, but he needed to please Jay and doubled down on his efforts to show Jay just how much he loved his cock and his body and his brain and everything else about him. Benji licked and sucked and nibbled Jay's hard cock until the man was whimpering and whining.

Jay pushed Benji's head and Benji followed the directions he gave and began focusing on Jay's balls. He wrapped one hand around the leaking cock and took one of Jay's balls into his mouth, licking and lightly sucking on it. When he was ready, he switched focus to the other ball and then focused on getting both balls in his mouth at the same time. He loved being choked by the fullness. He gagged around the balls and drool started to leak out of his mouth and onto the chair below. He pulled off Jay's balls and suckled on the leaking tip of his cock in an effort to catch his breath. It worked. Jay was making soothing motions with his hands in Benji's hair, but he still wasn't able to do more than whimper. Benji pulled off Jay's dick and moved down again, bypassing his balls to lick his taint. Jay bucked up at the unexpected touch but then quickly settled back down.

Benji didn't spend long teasing Jay's taint because he didn't want to miss the eruption that was sure to happen at any minute. He made his way back to Jay's cock and took him deep again. The vibrations thrummed through his chest and everywhere they touched and Benji wished that Jay could feel them. It made him sigh, but the sigh came out like a hum and that vibration had Jay spilling into his throat. Benji greedily swallowed him down and then pulled off, resting his head on Jay's bare thigh.

Before they had both fully caught their breaths, Jay pulled Benji off his knees and frantically pawed at his jeans. Benji took a step back and carefully stripped out of the pants, kicking off his shoes at the same time.

Gods, it's a good thing I didn't wear my boots today. Benji straddled Jay's leg and slowly began to grind his wet cunt against the top of Jay's thigh. He wrapped one hand around the back of Jay's neck and let the other rest on the chairback so he could balance himself as he rocked his hips back and forth. Ideally he'd have one of his grinders strapped to Jay's thigh but this would do for now. He thought about pulling Jay's corduroy pants back up and using the ridges on them to help stimulate his swollen clit. The thought had him picking up pace and he had no desire to stop even for the twenty seconds it would take to facilitate that. Jay's hands were around his hips, directing him to take longer and faster thrusts. Benji needed more of Jay connected with him. He moved his hands to the bottom of the blouse he was wearing and tore it off over his head. He made quick work of also removing his binder, and like he was reading Benji's mind, Jay leaned forward and enveloped one of his nipples in his mouth. Benji cried out and thrust faster. Jay reached below where Benji was grinding on his thigh and positioned his hand so it gave Benji something better to pleasure himself with.

Benji was getting so close, but he still needed more. Jay had been switching between his nipples, both breasts wet with sweat and saliva.

"Jay, turn your hand over. I need you in me," Benji directed. Jay did as instructed and flipped his hand over when Benji's hips pulled back. On his next thrust, Benji felt three of Jay's fingers enter his wet vagina and his clit struck the palm of Jay's hands. He cried out and began thrusting faster until the familiar sensation of his orgasm started climbing up his legs and he gushed over Jay's hand and lap. Jay swallowed his cry with a kiss, keeping his hand positioned under Benji where he was sure to feel the aftershocks rocketing through Benji's system.

After a moment, when the shocks began to slow, Jay pulled his hand out from under Benji and wrapped his arm around his waist, careful not to rest the wet hand directly on Benji's skin.

"So, I take it you missed me?" Jay asked in a light tone.

"Apparently," Benji mused.

Their eyes met and they started giggling again. Benji couldn't remember the last time he laughed so consistently with a person. He had friends whose company he enjoyed and they had the occasional laugh, but it wasn't anything like this.

Jay flicked his wrist and muttered an incantation that cleaned them both up. They got up off the chair and Benji magicked away any remnants of their cum and sweat. They slowly put themselves together, stealing soft kisses between putting their clothes back on or adjusting their hair and setting the space to rights.

When they were comfortable and confident that everything was back in order, Benji removed the enchantments from his door and the perimeter of the office and sat down on an extra wide chair next to Jay.

"How was your presentation?" he asked, happy to discuss their days now that his mind could focus on the conversation.

"It went well. I have a couple of colleagues interested in developing their own prototypes, so I'm working on drawing up a blueprint based on all of my research."

This surprised Benji. He was so used to having sketches on sketches on sketches and scaled models of his pieces that he couldn't imagine someone like Jay not having extensive notes and multiple blueprint drafts.

"You don't have that already?" he asked.

"Photographic memory, remember?"

"Oh right. I don't know how I forgot that."

"Your brain probably hasn't come back online after that world-shattering orgasm," Jay teased.

Benji laughed. "It was mind-blowing, that's for sure."

"How was your day? Did you get anywhere with the research for our bet?"

Benji thought about the work he had done so far. He shifted his theory from being able to feel all auras to being able to feel the auras of other aurals. He had a backup that he was somehow only able to feel the auras of those he was close to, but he wanted to rule out the larger category first.

"I've narrowed down the reach a bit, and I've got a meeting with Beryl and a couple of their friends who were gracious enough to volunteer their time. That's set up next week, so there's still time for you to beat me to the finish line on this one."

"Honestly, I think we're gonna be pretty neck-and-neck this time," Jay sighed, the day catching up to him as he leaned against Benji's shoulder. Benji moved his arm so it wrapped around him and Jay could snuggle up on his chest. Benji kissed the curls on the top of his head and just relaxed with the man he was falling for. Everything felt so domestic, and for once, that didn't scare him.

Benji was busy getting ready for midterms so he didn't have as much time to pop in on Jay as he would have liked. Thankfully, between their phones and the ancient intercollegiate messaging system, they were able to stay in near constant communication throughout the day.

Jay was also busy most days helping students and professors with research to prepare for their various papers and exams. He made a point to visit Benji on his lunch breaks and bring him treats from Jack's. Benji rarely had more than five minutes at a time to take a break, but on those few occasions where he had more like ten or fifteen, they made good use of the extra time. Jay enjoyed how he could get Benji hot and bothered through his messages and then take him apart and put him back together again in under ten minutes if he had to. Usually, those encounters resulted in Benji rushing off to a class and Jay being left to clean up after them, but he didn't mind. Especially when it meant he was able to taste Benji for the rest of the day. He often gloated about this to Benji during their nightly debriefs.

Benji made it to Thursday when he had his meeting with Beryl and their friends to test his theory about being able to connect with other aurals. He strode into the lecture hall with a couple of boxes of pizza and saw the small group of 5 graduate and undergraduate students waiting with his TA.

"Thank you all for coming. I brought lunch." He set the boxes down on the lecturer's desk and grabbed a slice before the students devoured the rest of them. Once everyone had their lunch, they gathered in a circle and focused their attention on Benji.

"Hi everyone, thank you again for coming. Long story short, I need your help. I was out with a friend"—He hesitated at the word "friend." It didn't feel enough to describe the relationship he and Jay had, but it would work in this context—"and we discovered something strange happening. I was able to feel his aura, or at least that's what we think was happening. Now I am not an aural, so this was a new experience. Over the last week or so, I've been trying to elicit similar results from other people I know. Unfortunately, I haven't had any success with other non-aurals. So I asked Beryl to bring along some friends who might be willing to help me determine if this new ability is able to manifest with any aural or if I have to have an existing relationship with them."

He waited as the group digested his words alongside the pizza. One of the younger undergrads looked particularly excited to be part of this experiment.

When Benji felt like enough time had passed, he continued. "Now, I don't believe there is any risk of harm with this, but I want you all to know that you are under no obligation to continue. You can just enjoy the pizza and leave, you can stick around and observe, or you can participate if you wish. There is no pressure and will be no repercussions if you decide not to take part."

This seemed to ease some of the students' minds. One of them politely excused himself, but stuck around to watch, while the other four plus Beryl decided they wanted to participate. Benji passed out a piece of paper asking them to write down their aura color, the aura color they saw for him, and then as he shook each of their hands in turn, he asked them to write down if they noticed any reaction: patterns, color mixing, avoidance, etc. He waited for them to fill out the first section of their sheets and placed five sheets of his own on the desk in front of him. His research sheets were a little different as they contained only two questions—*What is your relationship with the subject?* and *Was there a vibration noticed?*

When everyone was ready to start, he asked them to come up one by one, give their name and shake his hand. For the students he had never encountered before, he noted that there were no vibrations. When Beryl's best friend came and shook his hand, Benji noticed a shock that could easily be mistaken for static electricity, so he repeated the handshake and noted that it happened every time. When it was finally time for Beryl, Benji noticed that there was a comfortable humming vibration, more noticeable than any others, but nowhere near as intense as what he felt with Jay. As a precaution, Benji went back and shook hands with those who didn't illicit a reaction the first time and noticed that the results were the same.

He thanked them all and collected their sheets, ready to look at their side of the data. Beryl hung back as everyone else left.

"Vibratory aura patterns?" they asked.

"Yeah, it happened with Archivist Byrd a couple weeks ago when we were waiting in the teleport queue, and pretty much every time we've seen each other since," Benji admitted to his trusted TA.

"This is exciting, Prof. I've never heard of anything like it. We could be experiencing a new facet of magic develop right before our eyes, or well, my eyes, your life."

Benji hadn't really thought about it that way. This discovery would be bigger than just him and Jay. It could impact the world as they knew it.

"Thanks Beryl. I honestly haven't thought about global impact beyond my own life," Benji admitted.

Beryl clasped him on the shoulder and Benji took comfort in the faint hum of a vibration he felt at the reassurance.

"It will be okay. This isn't something to be scared about."

And with that little bit of comfort, Beryl scooped up their bag and headed out of the lecture hall. Benji took his papers and the empty pizza boxes with him back to his office where he could look everything over without being interrupted.

chapter sixteen

JAY'S HAND was starting to cramp with how much writing he'd been doing in the past few days. Normally, he'd just work on his computer, but it was easier to transcribe everything by hand so he could include the drawings he needed for his notes. He was by no means a talented artist, but his skills were sufficient enough for the crude illustrations he needed. *Maybe I should ask Benji to help*, he thought. He remembered the sketches of Alchvhybium that Benji had shown him when they first met and knew that he'd need to ask his paramour about helping him whenever he saw him next.

As if the thought of Benji was enough to summon him, the message board lit up with the alert of a new message. Jay knew it was from his professor as Benji was the only person to use the interdepartmental messaging service with him.

The message contained only two words:

Get Ready.

Jay's cock began to stir at the implication of the

message. He wasn't sure if he was more excited about the payoff from their bet or about the new information Benji had discovered.

Oh, who am I kidding? I can't wait for Benji to be inside me.

Jay wondered if he should go to find the professor or if he would come to Jay. Before he could decide, the door opened and a beaming Benji came striding in, beverages and treats from Jack's in hand.

"You spoil me," Jay said, taking the matcha and cookie. He set them down on the tea cart next to his desk and pulled Benji in for a kiss.

Benji hummed when their lips touched. It was sweet and made Jay wonder just what they were doing. He was falling for this man— his sweet gestures, his humor, his memory, everything about him made Jay long for something more. He broke off the kiss with the determination of finding out if his growing feelings were at all mutual.

"Benj, I..." he started, but got distracted when Benji pulled a stack of papers out of his bag.

"Hmm?" Benji asked. "What were you going to say?"

Benji put the papers on Jay's desk and Jay decided to wait before having the conversation about their relationship.

"It can wait. Tell me what you found."

"Are you sure?" Benji asked. Jay internally debated whether or not it was the right time for the conversation but ultimately decided against it.

"Yeah, I'm sure. This is more pressing."

"Okay," Benji took him at his word and Jay appreciated the trust. Benji spread out the information and gestured to it. "Take a look."

Jay studied the papers and saw that the bottom row was all in the same familiar script. Each column seemed to be paired with an aural's observations on top and Benji's on the bottom.

The ones who Benji claimed to have no prior relationship or significant interactions with all had a null reaction on his part. Those participants also noted that Benji's aura looked more of a pale butter yellow than what Jay usually saw. From their first meeting, Benji's aura glowed like sunshine and radiated with patterns Jay had never really seen before. It was enough to make him think Benji was special, but it hadn't ever seemed like such an anomaly before. Jay returned to the papers. The same aurals also noted no strange or abnormal reactions when they shook Benji's hand, even when some of them did it multiple times. Jay looked down at Benji's notes for those interactions. He felt no vibrations at their interactions, nothing out of the ordinary. It was the way things had always been with people before he met Jay.

Then Jay looked over the two pages with more notes than the others. One aural, a person named Steve, noted he had "previously met and interacted with Professor Rollins on a number of occasions, though their interactions were not of any significance." He noted that Benji's aura was a more standard yellow, similar to the center of a flower and contained a soft swirl pattern. Upon their handshake, Steve wrote that their auras swirled around each other but didn't truly blend.

Jay looked down at his notes of the interaction and was surprised to see that Benji felt a "static electricity-like shock" each time they shook hands. They replicated the handshake multiple times with the same reaction each time. Jay's head was starting to swim with alternative theories.

The last paper had a name Jay recognized: Beryl,

Benji's teaching assistant. He sat at his desk and read Beryl's observations.

While I always knew there was something different and special about Professor Rollins, I never paid much thought in how it might manifest. As the professor's teaching assistant, I have a fairly involved professional relationship with him, though I'd like to say it has progressed to a bit of a friendship over the years. When I first met Professor Rollins, I didn't think much of his aura, but as I got to know him, I noticed various shapes and patterns within his aura, along with a deepening of the yellow color. As of today, it appears more like a warm yellow with golden undertones that are evident in various patterns, primarily swirls.

Jay kept reading to see what their interactions were like from Beryl's perspective.

When Professor Rollins and I shook hands today, I noticed that our auras mingled. It wasn't something I've noticed before, as my aura has yellow undertones. I paid specific attention to it this time and noticed that my orange aura glowed more golden where our hands made contact. I also noticed that the swirling patterns of Professor Rollins' aura were more noticeable the closer we got to our contact. They took on a bit of an orange tint which made them stand out.

Jay hurriedly skimmed over Benji's notes and then looked up at him.

"This is incredible," he exclaimed.

"I agree," Benji said with a smile. "It seems I need to have some sort of established connection with an aural before I'm able to feel their aura, and the stronger that connection, the more intense the vibration."

"But your aura and mine interacted from the first moment we met," Jay admitted.

"It did? I didn't know that."

"It did. The first time we met, our auras reached for each other, and then when we touched, they blended together to make this gorgeous deep green."

"Fascinating," Benji said as he perched on the armrest of one of the chairs in front of Jay's desk. "I wonder why that happened."

"Maybe something in the universe knew we'd be important to each other."

"I like that line of thinking. But I don't remember any sort of buzz or shock happening before our date night."

"Hmm." Jay pondered why that might be but nothing was coming to mind. "This is all new to the world. In all my studies and reading, I've never heard of someone feeling another person's aura. And you're sure it has to be with another aural?"

"Yes, I casually noted my interactions with other people I encountered throughout the last week or so and nothing happened except with these two." Benji pointed at the papers for Beryl and Steve.

"What was the catalyst? Why were you able to start

feeling auras?" Jay looked up when Benji didn't answer right away.

Benji looked deep in contemplation and Jay thought he saw a hint of anxiety etched in the expression on his face. Jay waited.

"I have a theory, but I'm a little nervous to put it out there."

"I won't judge you, no matter how wild or unlikely it might be." Jay hoped his light tone would ease some of Benji's nerves.

"Well…" Benji started and then paused. "Well, I think it might have something to do with my feelings towards a person."

Jay held his breath. He didn't want to read into what Benji was saying, but he also felt the hope rising in his chest.

"With Steve, I'm cordial, but it's casual. There really aren't feelings there other than considering him a friendly acquaintance. Beryl, on the other hand, is someone I consider a friend despite our professional working relationship. We have a good rapport that has been built over the past two years of working together. And then there's you…"

Benji stepped over to Jay and placed his hands on either side of Jay's waist. His voice continued barely louder than a whisper.

"The first time I saw you, Jay, something in my chest leapt and I had a feeling you were going to be someone important to me. At the time, I wrote it off as you being the one to help me solve my seemingly elusive problem. But then I got to know you more and my feelings grew more intense. And then we had a memorable and wonderful afternoon of mind-blowing, world-shattering sex and my heart gave in. The next day, when I saw you before our date, you were talking to Felix, joking about something, and then you looked over at me and I was a goner. I realized that I was falling in love with you."

Jay's heart soared. Benji was falling for him, too. Jay wanted to write a declaration in the sky for the world to see, but he was tongue-tied and at a loss for words for the first time in his life, so he did the only thing that made sense in the moment. He pulled Benji close and kissed him.

His eyes might have been closed, but Jay's mind produced a cacophony of stars and explosions of color. It was like their auras were seeping into his mind and putting on a show that only he could see. Benji was falling in love with him. He deepened their kiss with the thought. Both men were grasping at each other; Jay felt Benji's hands slide down his back to just below his ass, and the tug that followed closed any distance that might have still been between them.

Benji hummed and the vibration Jay felt intensified the sensation of the kiss. He wasn't sure if Benji was intentionally trying to mimic the feeling of their auras mixing, but Jay wasn't complaining. He wished he could experience more of what Benji felt, and he wanted to be able to share the colors with the man who would be able to appreciate them from an artist's perspective.

When they finally broke apart, both men looked dazed and a bit drunk on each other.

As soon as he had his wits about him, Jay spoke the words he wanted to say as soon as he saw Benji walk in.

"I'm falling for you, too."

chapter seventeen

BENJI COULDN'T BELIEVE what he'd heard. Jay was falling in love with him, too. Beyond validating his theory of why his world vibrated whenever he was around the beautiful man, his heart was ecstatic. He wanted to whisk him away and spend hours or days pleasuring him and catering to his every desire. He wanted to serve him and submit to him and do anything and everything Jay wanted.

"Come home with me?" he pleaded.

Jay smiled at him and nodded enthusiastically.

Benji took his hand and left everything where it was on Jay's desk. They could come back to get it in the morning. Right now, they had a teleport to take.

Benji watched as Jay cast an enchantment to lock his office and then they practically raced to the teleportation circle that would take them down to the library atrium. It was hard not to giggle at their childish behavior. They couldn't stop touching each other and Benji felt like an eight-year-old palling around with his best friend. He felt giddy. When they were clear to move off the teleportation circle, they both composed themselves among the students enough to mask any behavior that might look suspicious and briskly walked out of the library. Benji was grateful that Felix wasn't at the desk today otherwise they might have been held up talking to them.

They made it to the university's off-campus teleport room and were relieved to find the line was short. As staff, they were able to bypass most of the formalities and Benji scanned his ID badge twice to denote that he was going to his base teleport and there were two people.

"I thought you didn't like teleporting home," Jay joked in a whisper that made the vibrations radiate all along Benji's body.

"I said I only do it when I'm in a rush, and Jay, I'm not wasting any more time," Benji purred and then gave Jay a peck on the cheek.

They stood in the center of the sigil and waited for it to activate. Benji closed his eyes as the familiar tingles started to crawl up his legs and when he opened them again, they were in the lobby of his apartment building.

"Welcome to my home," Benji held out his hand to take Jay's as they stepped off the sigil onto the marble floor.

"It's fancy," Jay mused.

"It's old," Benji corrected.

"Vintage," Jay offered.

"Antique."

"Retro."

They went back and forth with their synonyms as Benji led Jay to an elevator bank. The polished nature of the lobby slowly faded as the more dated parts of the building started to show through.

"Management likes to put a good foot forward for visitors and prospective tenants, but once you get into the nitty gritty of the building, you'll find that it's just… average."

"Average isn't bad." Jay looked at some of the details

on the walls next to the elevator. "They could have made it beige and boring, at least they seemed to keep some of the original touches."

"Very true," Benji agreed, pulling Jay into his arms and dipping him into a kiss.

The elevator dinged, the doors sliding open, and they laughed and stood back upright. Benji ushered Jay inside and pressed the button for the third floor.

The elevator let out to a hallway with a blue and green carpet. They turned left and walked about halfway down until they got to apartment 3G. Benji dispelled the enchantment keeping it magically locked and then used his key to unlock it the mundane way.

"It's a little bit overkill," he admitted as Jay watched. "But usually if someone is trying to break in, they won't have the skills to undo both locks, and if they do, they'll be pissed when they open everything up and find I don't have anything worth taking."

He swung the door open to reveal a fairly tidy, if not a little chaotic, one-bedroom apartment. He let Jay take it in and hoped that he wasn't turned off by his eclectic taste. Benji loved color, and his decor showed that. The sofa was a bright cobalt blue with golden-yellow accented pillows and an amethyst-purple throw blanket draped on the back.

He waited as Jay looked around the space, breath held in anticipation of his reaction.

"This is so perfectly you," Jay observed as his hand felt the fabric of the woven throw blanket. "It's fantastic."

Benji's heart warmed. He didn't usually bring people back to his apartment after a string of visitors called his decor "a bit of an eyesore" and other disheartening remarks. When Jay walked past him again, Benji reached out and pulled him close. The hum of the vibration pulsing between them amped up the heat and tension that had cooled slightly with their commute.

"Dance with me?" Benji asked. Jay nodded so he snapped his fingers and flicked his hand in the direction of the stereo. The soft plucking of an acoustic guitar echoed around the room. Benji slid his hand to Jay's waist, and when Jay did the same to him, he instinctively stepped closer. They clasped their other hands together and Benji took the first step. He lead Jay in a simple box step for the first few bars, but as the music began to swell, they became more adventurous with their footwork. Benji let himself get lost in the moment, staring into the galaxies of copper and blue that were Jay's irises. As the music crescendoed, he spun Jay away from him and when he returned, their lips met in a kiss that sent a shockwave of tremors radiating from them.

In that moment, Benji felt the world shift. He hadn't realized that he had closed his eyes at some point, but when he opened them, there was a new world of color surrounding them.

"I… I can feel you," Jay exclaimed breathlessly.

"I can see you," Benji laughed in reply. "Your colors, I mean."

Benji watched as the colors around them swirled and mixed, continuing the dance they had abandoned. The deep blue of Jay's aura mixed with his sunshine golden yellow to make rich tones of green. He still felt the vibrations, but now he could see where the shapes contained in his own aura affected the steadiness of Jay's. The shapes each had a unique vibration that pulsed at the interaction. In some instances, it seemed as if Jay's aura was being coaxed to come and play with Benji's.

Benji needed to explore this new revelation further. He took Jay's hand, watching as his yellow aura sparked with excitement against Jay's blue. He lead them into his bedroom, and laid Jay down on the bed before straddling him.

"I need you," Benji pleaded.

"I need you, too." Jay's words pierced his heart and the vibrations and golden glow intensified so brightly it momentarily filled the entire room.

Jay's hands began tugging at the hem of Benji's shirt, encouraging him to take it off. He scooted back so they were both able to sit up and Jay slid the shirt over Benji's head. In turn, Benji undressed Jay from the waist up, plopping his shirt and hoodie on top of Benji's discarded blouse. Benji grasped the bottom of his binder and removed it next.

Jay wrapped his hands around Benji and began gently rubbing his back. The vibrations they felt at the soft touch made them both shudder. Benji was already turned on, but this touch brought him closer to the edge than he'd been all night.

He threw his head back and lost himself in the sensation. Jay continued drawing maps and indexes on his back and Benji began to slowly rock back and forth, desperate for any sort of friction.

Jay stilled Benji's hips and rolled them over. He slid off Benji and the bed. Benji watched with haze-filled eyes as Jay removed his own pants and then began to remove Benji's. He lifted his hips, making it a little easier for Jay to slide his jeans and underwear down. Jay stared, heat increasing in his eyes, as Benji began to touch himself. He was already so wet. Jay collapsed on his knees and watched as Benji's fingers teased his clit and stroked the folds of his labia. He longed for Jay to take over and dominate him again, but Jay was mesmerized. Benji resolved to put on the best show he could. He watched as Jay's blue aura darkened to a midnight shade closer to black than he'd ever seen before. Jay was absentmindedly and slowly stroking his cock, eyes blown wide from his own arousal. He licked his lips and Benji summoned him forward.

Faster than lightning, Jay's face was between his legs and he began feasting on Benji's body. He licked up the sides of Benji's labia and sucked on his swollen clit, teasing every bit of it he could get his mouth around. Right when Benji felt himself ascending to the edge again, Jay pulled off and started tongue fucking his hole. He alternated between plunging his tongue in Benji's vagina and flicking his clit until Benji started to float off the bed with the ecstasy. He was only hovering an inch or two in the air, but Jay put his arm over Benji's plump belly anyway. Benji had never experienced this before. He'd heard stories of a connection between partners so strong that magic was uncontrollable, but he thought those were fairy tales.

Jay stood and, slowly, Benji floated back down to the mattress. Jay crawled up beside him.

"You made me float," Benji said with a smile.

"You changed my aura."

"Has that ever happened to you before?" Benji was still on edge but didn't want the night to wrap up too quickly, so he began taking slow breaths and focusing on the conversation rather than the vibrations pulsing from where their bodies were touching and where he could still feel the phantom of Jay's mouth on him.

"No," Jay admitted. "Well, at least not that intensely. There are usually minor fluctuations with intense emotions, but nothing as deep as this." He paused and stoked Benji's hair. "You're actually the first person I've ever seen with an aura that has patterns and changes hue based on your emotions. It's beautiful."

Benji laid there and let Jay's comments sink in. He

hadn't ever felt special or unique in that way. He'd always felt different from most of his peers. Being trans had always set him apart from most of the people he knew growing up. Being perceived one way, but knowing you truly exist as someone else, set him up for a lifetime of self-reflection and gave him the tools to sit with discomfort. Whenever someone would say things about him marching to the beat of his own drum or being special in the past, it was always laced with a tone of mockery, but right now, as Jay explained how he was different and told him he was beautiful, Benji felt truly seen for the first time in his life.

He rolled over on his side and faced Jay. His eyes scanned everything they could take in—Jay's sandy brown curls, his button nose and wet lips, the eyes that met Benji in his dreams, his kissable chin and jawline, the long neck that Benji loved to taste. There wasn't a part of Jay he didn't want to explore and worship.

Jay made Benji feel seen and now he wanted to return the favor.

"I see you in my dreams," he started. He brushed his fingers through Jay's curls. "The curls of your hair show up in patterns left by waves on the beach."

He kissed Jay's forehead and cheeks. "Your face brings me hope in the darkest of nightmares and elevates the joy of my best dreams. It brings me comfort when I close my eyes."

He let his fingertips glide over Jay's eyebrows and rest alongside his eyes. "Your eyes are like clusters of stars and galaxies untraversed. I find my thoughts drift to them when I'm awake and my subconscious visits those far off places when I sleep."

He kissed Jay's chin and nuzzled into his neck. "I find my best comfort and sleep when I imagine you next to me." He felt Jay swallow and glanced up at him. Moisture was starting to pool at the corners of his eyes, but Benji continued when he saw that Jay was also smiling.

"Your mind enraptures me. You take joy in the research you do and you constantly strive to keep learning. You don't put on airs when someone starts talking about something you already know about. You listen patiently and let others take the lead. You make people feel important."

Benji punctuated his speech with a kiss to Jay's still wet lips. He tasted himself on them, but beyond that surface taste was something distinctly Jay. Benji sighed as they broke the kiss.

"Benji, I…" Jay started and then paused to wipe his eyes. "Thank you."

He smiled over at Benji and they briefly got lost in each other's eyes again. Benji rolled to his back and Jay tucked himself into his side. This wasn't at all how Benji had imagined the night going, but he wouldn't change a single moment.

chapter eighteen

JAY'S MIND was content to stay in Benji's arms for the rest of forever, but his dick was also aching from the lack of release. After a while of comfortable snuggling and light kisses, the urgency grew to an unavoidable nuisance.

Wishing he had his rock for comfort, Jay's hand found the sheet and he started rubbing it between his fingers. Without turning to face Benji, he asked "Did you ever make a decision?"

"About what?" Benji questioned back.

"About the bet. Well, about the payoff from the bet." Jay closed his eyes hoping that Benji's answer would align with what he needed right now. As much as he would love to sink into Benji's tight, wet hole, he wanted to be taken and fucked into the mattress.

"I did"—Jay held his breath as Benji paused—"I want to top you first and then right before you're ready to come, I want you to take me in both holes."

Jay let out a little moan at the thought of Benji being stuffed full and letting him control their orgasms again. The trust that this man placed in him was powerful. He hoped he could fulfill Benji's fantasy.

"Yes, yes, let's do that," he enthusiastically agreed when his mind slowed down enough to let him speak.

Benji kissed him quickly and then got off the bed.

"Do you want to use condoms?" he asked. "I'm on birth control and have been getting preventative shots. I can also show you my latest test. It's negative across the board."

Jay shook his head. "I'm also negative. If you're comfortable forgoing them, I want to feel you all around me."

Benji gave him a dark and hungry look, "I can't wait to feel you in me and for you to fill me in every way."

Jay shuddered. "Gods yes. Get what you need and then get back here, please."

"Yes, sir," Benji teased. Fuck, his submission, even when he was being playful and bratty about it, turned Jay on. He couldn't wait to make Benji squirm, but first, he was going to enjoy being stuffed full and fucked with the strap-on Benji was bringing back to the bed.

Benji slipped on the harness that held the dildo in place. Jay looked at the man before him with his beautiful breasts, hairy chest, wet pussy, and the cock that he couldn't wait to have stuffed in his ass. His mouth watered and he let his dominant side take over.

"Are you ready, pet?" he asked. He watched Benji carefully. The golden yellow of his aura changed to a deep ochre and the vibrations gave off the feeling of anticipation. Benji sunk to his knees next to the bed and Jay gave him an approving smile and a touch on the cheek.

"Good boy. Now I want you to open me up. Use your tongue, use your fingers, use the lube. Make sure I'm good and ready because you're going to stuff me full of your cock until I tell you to stop. You are not allowed to come until I'm inside of you. Is that understood, pet?"

"Yes, sir." Benji nodded enthusiastically.

Jay flipped to his stomach, pulled his knees under him, and rocked his hips back so his hole was right where Benji would need it.

"Whenever you're ready, pet."

He let his head fall to the duvet and breathed in the scent of Benji that permeated the soft fabric, chewing on his lower lip in anticipation. When he finally felt the hot breath of Benji's mouth hovering right over his hole, he wiggled his hips a little bit as an encouragement for Benji to dive in. It worked. Jay moaned as Benji's tongue swiped across his hole. Hearing Jay make noises seemed to spur Benji on. He went back a few more times with simple, teasing licks across the rim of Jay's hole.

"More, please, Benj," Jay urged. He wanted to be filled and fucked. He wanted his professor to teach him a few things about rimming.

He stopped whining when Benji's hands gripped his hips. He moved Jay into a position that allowed Benji to access him more easily from his knees. Jay yet again held his breath and waited. This time, Benji started at the base of his balls and licked up his taint. When he got to his hole again, he nipped at it before plunging his tongue inside. With Benji's confidence came a surge of vibrations unlike anything Jay had ever felt. It was almost as if Benji's tongue was a vibrator. The sensation made him tense initially, but Benji was patient and kept licking at Jay's rim, sucking and gently biting with his teeth, until Jay's body relaxed.

Jay got used to the vibrations and the pulsing actually helped him open up quicker once he got over the initial shock of it. Just as Jay was getting lulled into a headspace that made him start to feel as if he was going to float, Benji replaced his tongue with a lube-slicked finger.

Jay moaned in pleasure as Benji's finger slid deeply inside him. He began to rock back and forth, taking Benji's finger down past the second knuckle.

"Are you ready for more?" Benji asked, his voice husky.

"Yes, please, pet. I need you to open me faster," he managed to say despite his hazy mind.

Benji popped open the lube cap and squirted more on his fingers. A second finger joined the first and Jay's hole practically sucked both tips in. It took a little work for Benji to go deeper than the first knuckle with both fingers, but he was skilled. And the vibration was still adding an intensity neither of them could have imagined. Jay thought he would see stars before the night was over.

"Feels so good," Jay encouraged.

Benji wrapped his free arm around Jay's waist and gripped his cock. He gave it a quick squeeze at the base and then wiped some of Jay's precum from the tip. Jay looked back as Benji brought the precum to his lips and moaned when he tasted it.

"You're delicious," Benji told him, still fucking him open with both fingers. Jay whimpered. He was trying to be patient, but it was getting more and more difficult. He was bordering on desperation to get Benji to stick his dick inside him.

"Soon, sir. You're going to be ready after this next finger."

Jay felt a third digit join the other two and sighed. He was starting to finally feel the fullness he craved. When Benji deemed him ready, he braced himself as the three fingers and their vibrations pulled out from his hole. He could feel it pulsing, trying desperately to pull them back in.

Benji didn't wait long before lining up his dick to Jay's entrance. Jay's fingers clutched at the sheets as Benji began taking shallow thrusts. Jay was about to take over and make Benji lie on the bed so he could fuck himself on the dildo, but right before he could make his first move, Benji pulled Jay's hips back slowly as he moved his forward. Benji's dick sunk all the way into Jay and he sighed in relief as he could feel Benji's hips hit his ass.

Benji waited for Jay to adjust and stroked Jay's cock languidly.

When Jay felt like his body was ready, he gave Benji a two-word command, "Rail me."

Benji dropped Jay's cock and gripped his hips tightly. He pulled out and thrust back in with a force that made Jay feel the dick in his throat. Jay loved being handled this way. He would take things slowly and gently for his partner and still find his own pleasure, but when it was his turn to be taken, he loved it rough and fast.

The dildo Benji was using felt almost indistinguishable from any other dick Jay had encountered. He cried out each time Benji thrust in and hit his prostate. The vibrations from their auras made the sensation so intense that Jay was afraid he'd lose his vision. He was rock hard and leaking all over Benji's rosetted blue duvet.

"So good," he cried the next time Benji pegged his hole.

Benji's return was a cry of ecstasy which snapped Jay back from the edge. He still wanted to get inside Benji. He unclenched his fingers from the duvet and moved one of his hands to encompass Benji's.

"Pet, how are you doing? Are you close?" he asked.

"Yes! I'm so close. Sir, please. I need—I need you," Benji responded. Jay felt a twinge of guilt at not staying attuned to his partner.

"I'm sorry, love. You did so great. You can rest now. I'll take care of you," Jay assured him. He moved his hand back to the sheet and braced himself for the emptiness that would come when Benji withdrew his dildo. He almost wished he had brought a butt plug or something to keep him full while he stuffed Benji.

Benji was plastered to his back, catching his breath. When Jay felt him start to move and get up, he began to panic.

"Wait, don't pull out yet," he urged. Benji wrapped his arms around Jay's stomach and kissed his shoulder blade.

"What's wrong?"

"Do you…" Jay could feel a blush heating his cheeks and saw his aura start to turn a light shade of blue. He took a deep breath and then asked, "Do you have a plug or something? I'm not ready to be empty yet."

His fingers played with the duvet cover, rubbing it between his fingers as he waited for Benji to answer.

"Yeah, I do. I'll have to pull out to get it. Is that okay?"

Jay nodded and then braced again as Benji retreated from his back, pulling the dildo out with him. Jay tried to focus on his erection and still leaking cock rather than the ache of emptiness he felt in his ass. He gave himself a couple tugs to keep things hard.

Benji's hurried footsteps signaled his return and Jay sighed when he felt Benji's calloused hand return to his thigh.

"I've got this one for you. It's one of my favorites. I just wanted to give it an extra clean real quick before you used it." Benji showed Jay the sparkly purple plug. It looked delectably thick but not so girthy that Jay would be uncomfortable or have issues pleasing Benji. He smiled and Benji squeezed his hip. Jay's ass fit around the plug hungrily and the flared base sat snugly in his crack.

"I wish it vibrated so it would feel like you were still in me."

Benji laughed. "We'll have to look for one of those for next time." He laid down next to Jay and ran his curls through Jay's sweat-dampened hair.

Jay let his eyes rove over Benji's beautiful body. He had taken off his strap-on, which Jay was slightly disappointed about. He fantasized about giving Benji a blowjob while he was wearing it. He'd just have to wait and do that at another time if it was something Benji would enjoy.

Jay reached out his hand and caressed one of Benji's breasts, twirling the nipple between his fingers. He firmly squeezed the other one and then let his hand travel down to the wetness between Benji's thighs. Jay lazily sunk his fingers in Benji's cunt and felt just how wet and turned on he was. He played with Benji for a while, drinking in all of his little gasps and the moans he tried to bite back.

"On your side, pet," Jay ordered.

Benji rolled so his back was facing Jay. Jay looked over at the bedside table and grabbed one of the thrusting dildos that Benji had laid out. He lubed it up with one hand while he continued to tease Benji's clit and front hole. When the dildo was ready, he moved it into position and drew his hand back to Benji's ass. He turned on the dildo so it started with some shallow thrusts and magicked it to stay in position so he could focus on opening Benji's other hole.

He situated Benji with one leg bent and his knee in the air, kissed him on the neck and then slid down to the edge of the bed where he could open him up. Jay began by teasing his hole with his fingers that were still wet from Benji's vagina. He popped the tip of his middle finger in at the same time the dildo thrust out of Benji's front hole. Benji gasped and reached up to hold the railings of his headboard.

Jay smiled and kept working his finger shallowly in and

out of Benji's hole in tandem with the dildo. By the time he had worked two fingers into him, Benji was panting and squirming. Jay had to still his movement with a hand on his hip. Jay's cock was angry and leaking so much that he knew it wouldn't take long for him to blow once he got inside Benji. He repositioned the dildo so it was fully seated in Benji's cunt, thrusting deeply into him and never fully pulling out.

He lined his freshly lubed-up dick with Benji's hole and slowly pushed in. He got a little way in and waited for Benji to adjust. When Benji started squirming again, he pushed in further. They repeated that a few times until Jay was fully seated inside Benji's ass. He could feel the thrusting dildo and the shocks it was giving Benji. The aura vibration between them right now was somehow more intense than it had been earlier.

Jay wrapped his body around Benji, so his chest was snug with Benji's back. He moved his hands up and started playing with Benji's breasts, squeezing them and flicking and twisting the nipples. Benji cried out in ecstasy and Jay was encouraged to keep going.

Their auras were mixed so deeply that there was only a small golden lining on the outside. The rest of it was a deep blue-green. Jay knew he would never be the same after Benji. He couldn't imagine an "after-Benji." He would do anything to keep this man forever. Right now, that meant giving him the best orgasm of his life.

Jay began to move his hips, gyrating and thrusting so that Benji was full and stuffed the way he wanted. He let the sensation of their bodies, the toys, and the vibrations wash over them. The tightness of Benji's ass gripped his dick perfectly. He could feel Benji tensing and he rose with him.

When Benji was nearing tears from the pleasure, Jay

whispered in his ear, "Come for me, pet," and then nipped his earlobe. With a loud shout, Benji's orgasm rocketed through him and a pulse wave shocked through the room, knocking over pillows and tilting artwork on the wall. As Benji's ass tightened from his orgasm, Jay came with his own cry. The aftershocks from Benji's orgasm milked Jay through the end of his. With the last of his energy, he turned off the thrusting dildo and tossed it onto the bed.

Jay tried hard to keep himself from falling asleep right there, the smell of their cum, musk, and sweat mixing in the air, the comfort of the man he loved resting in his arms.

Despite his best efforts, Jay dozed off, but thankfully it wasn't for long. Benji was asleep in his arms, and Jay's soft dick had slid out of him, but they were sticky with sweat that was beginning to crust over. Jay was torn between his desire to care for Benji and clean things up and his longing to stay in bed. He was just about to roll out of bed when he remembered that he could use magic and clean them up. The orgasm had truly fried his brain.

Benji didn't stir as Jay carefully moved the toys over to a towel that he summoned from the bathroom—they could clean those later. He then cast an incantation to clean up the mess they'd made on the duvet and summoned another warm, damp wash cloth to clean up Benji and another for himself. Jay tossed both of those over to the laundry basket and then curled back up with Benji, kissing the nape of his neck as he did.

When he came to consciousness again, he felt both suns shining in through the window. At some point he had rolled onto his back and gotten under the covers. He reached his hand out to find Benji, but no one was there. He felt a weight on his chest though and blinked open his eyes to see a small calico cat staring at him with a judgmental expression on her face.

"You must be Fjona," Jay groggily said, hoping he wouldn't offend her with his morning breath. "I'm Jay. Benji has told me all about you. Hopefully he's told you a few things about me too."

She stared back. He felt like he was visiting his great-aunt again. That woman could get a confession out of a mafia Don.

"I'm guessing you're wondering what my intentions are?"

She settled in further as if inviting him to continue because she wouldn't be moving until he did.

"Well, I'm falling in love with him—no, that's not right. I'm pretty sure I'm past the falling stage at this point. I'm in love with him. I want to spend my days finding all the ways to make him happy and bring color into his life. I want to care for him and make it impossible for him to think that he is not loved and adored. I want him to know without a shadow of a doubt that he is special and unique in the best ways. That he is the highlight of my day and the sun my universe revolves around."

Seemingly satisfied with that answer, Fjona made a noise that sounded like a mix between a chirp and a purr and then hopped off Jay and stretched out her body before trotting out of the room.

Jay listened and heard the clanking of pots and pans along with some soft jazz playing out in the kitchen area. He grabbed his boxers from the mess on the floor and threw them on before walking out to see the man who captured his heart.

Benji was standing in the kitchen dancing around and

making a delicious-smelling breakfast. Jay noticed his joy first and his aura second. He gasped and Benji turned around to face him.

"What's wrong?" He asked with concern.

"Your aura. It changed. It's..." Jay walked closer and studied it. "You're not full yellow anymore. I mean your sunshine is still there, but just on the edges. The core is a dark green. And your swirls are... my blue."

Benji smiled and kissed Jay. "We match, then." The vibration humming at a steady and comforting purr much like Fjona who was sitting in the corner on a cat tree Jay had missed the night before. He held out his hand and saw that he indeed had the same aura color and markings as Benji.

"I've never seen anything like this before," he admitted with awe.

"Well then you better hurry up and eat breakfast because it sounds like you've got some research to do." Benji pinched his side playfully and went to go retrieve the plates of bacon, cheesy scrambled eggs, and toast.

They ate in a comfortable silence. Jay's head was spinning with too many thoughts. Benji was sitting on a stool next to him, scribbling in his notebook. He kept looking back at Jay and smiling.

"Why do you keep looking at me like that?"

"Because I have a crush on you, but shhh don't tell." Benji laughed and then took their empty plates over to the kitchen sink to be cleaned.

Benji went to go take his shower first and Jay did the dishes leaving them to dry in the draining rack. When Benji came back out, Jay went in and took a quick shower. Benji had left him out a toothbrush to use and when he came back to grab his clothes, Benji had taken care of cleaning them off too.

"I'm really good with that particular cleaning enchantment," he teased, referencing the first time they had seen each other and Benji had been a mess from being in his studio.

Jay chuckled as he got dressed. When they were both ready, they clasped hands and walked out of the apartment. Jay waited patiently as Benji locked everything up. They made their way outside to a gorgeous day where the suns were both shining and the birds were chirping. Suddenly, Jay felt something between his feet.

He looked down to see Fjona was rubbing up against his legs affectionately.

"Looks like she approves of you," Benji interpreted. "Here, give her one of these and you'll have a best friend for life." He pulled a dried sardine out of a tin he kept in his pocket and handed it to Jay.

Jay bent down and Fjona snatched it out of his fingers before he was done presenting it to her. She chirped a thanks and trotted off to do whatever she did during the day.

Benji and Jay walked hand in hand toward the forest and back to school.

chapter nineteen

Two Months Later

BENJI PUT down the plastic paint spatula he used to get fine details in his sculpture and stood back. The project was almost done. All that remained was waiting for the paper pulp to dry and the alchemical reactions to finalize.

Working on finding the correct formula to essentially bring back an extinct element had garnered a lot of attention once the word got out and Benji had the deans of the transmutation and alchemy schools along with the president of the university and the board chair all stopping by for daily check-ins.

After his first successful test, he and Jay had celebrated all night before telling anyone. Benji smiled at the memory. His boyfriend made him happier than he'd ever imagined he could be.

Benji wished Jay could have been here for the sculpture's completion, but he was locked away in Scarpial B putting the finishing touches on his speech for a conference in Amhritran, where he would present his findings on the newly discovered vibratory aura. Benji was going with him for support and to help with the demonstration, but Jay was doing all the heavy lifting.

It had been two months since their auras had mixed and not much had changed. Jay once admitted that he missed Benji's sunshine but then Benji pointed out that Jay always carried it with him since it was the lining of both of their auras. The eating out and rimming Benji received after were just one way Jay showed his love of that idea. Jay's aura was still the only one Benji was able to see, and he was curious if Jay had found an answer to that yet. He'd been looking, but there hadn't been any breakthroughs.

Benji looked over at the message board that had become their default way of communicating while they were in their offices and saw it had a message. He walked over and read it:

Heading over in 5, I'll bring treats. Got something for you to see.

Benji heard his stomach rumbling and checked the time on the clock over his chalkboard. It was nearly six o'clock. He'd been working for five hours without a break. The time blindness often happened when he was lost in a project.

The formula and process for creating the Alchvhybium was time consuming and tedious. There were only a couple times when he was able to stop and take breaks. Once the chemical paper had been blended with the water to create the pulp, he had a limited amount of time to use it before it became unstable and impossible to work with.

He glanced over at it now and watched as the hard outer shell that encased the magma-like substance started to turn clear as it continued to harden. Figuring out the correct ratio of heating enchantments so that the exterior was finished before the central substance had any chance to dry out was one of the toughest challenges with this project. The breakthrough came when Jay tried to make some chocolate chip muffins that ended up turning into an unbaked chocolate chip lava cake muffin. Benji realized that by adding a small layer of high heat runes to the paper that would be used on the exterior, he was able to essentially sear the outside and leave the inside to stay in its more liquid form and not dry out fully. He also had to source his water carefully. He couldn't use the standard water from the tap like with his other projects. He had to use water from a well in a cave. It had to be transported so that light didn't touch it before it was finished. As a result, Benji did much of his carving in a dark room. One of his fellow alchemy professors had perfected a dark room setup for his practical photography application, so Benji was able to enlist his help in equipping his own workspace.

Benji had placed a thick velvet curtain across the entry way to his office to block out any ambient light that might make its way in whenever the door was opened. After checking to make sure that it was fully drawn, Benji walked over to where the statue was drying. The onyx and copper portions of it were slower to dry, so he had started those a few days ago. The Alchvhybium's exterior was almost fully transparent and had adhered to the copper successfully. There were still some sections of the copper that would take a few more days to dry because they had to be attached to the top of the Alchvhybium, so Benji'd had to wait to add them today.

Every part of this project had challenged him, but it was a breakthrough for both modern day science and magic. Much was still unknown about Alchvhybium from a practical standpoint, but he had already sent some samples off to colleagues in other departments and a few trusted friends at different institutions to see what they could discover.

Benji heard the door open and close and then the curtain rustled at the edge of the room. He knew it could only be Jay, as the protective enchantment he had placed on the office to guard the Alchvhybium had been spelled to let in Jay, and Jay alone. Anyone else who wanted to be let in had to be granted entry by Benji.

Jay walked through the opening between the curtain and the wall with drinks and food in hand. Benji did a quick cleaning incantation to make sure he didn't have any alchemical flecks on him and then went over to grab his items and a kiss from his boyfriend.

They had decided on their walk back to the university the morning after their first night in Benji's apartment that they wanted to be together in a defined relationship.

"I have one more bet," Benji had said.

"What's that?" Jay had asked with a twinkle in his eye.

"I bet that we'd make a great couple." Benji had turned his grinning face towards Jay and saw that Jay looked at him with love and admiration.

"Well, I certainly wouldn't bet against that," Jay had replied.

"Boyfriends?"

"Boyfriends," Jay had agreed. They'd sealed their commitment with a kiss only a few steps away from the first place Jay had kissed Benji.

The kiss Benji gave Jay now was just as sweet. Their passion for each other was growing stronger every day. The buzzing from their auras was so in sync that they barely noticed it except under times of heightened passion or emotion.

They sat down on a velvet loveseat that Benji had procured once Jay started spending more time in his office.

He watched as Jay ran his fingers along the fabric. Jay was a tactile person he had noticed over the past few months. He was constantly playing with things and touching different textures. He showed Benji the stone that he kept in his pocket to fidget with and Benji had since gone out of his way to find or make other objects Jay could fidget with. There was quite the collection growing on a dedicated shelf in their apartment.

Benji had asked Jay to move in with him after they spent the weekend apart for an aural retreat and he hadn't gotten more than ten hours of sleep between the three days Jay was away. Jay was more than happy to agree as he had only amassed eight hours himself.

Benji sipped his iced beverage and basked in the comfort of sitting close to the man he loved.

"I have something to show you," Jay said, breaking the silence after he had finished his treat.

"Oh, what's that?"

Jay reached into his bag and pulled out a book. It was another of Edwina's diaries.

"You found another one?"

"Yes, this is her last one I think. The entries are all dated right before she retreated from public life."

He handed it to Benji who read,

I have found something truly special in my Aimee. She brings a peace and comfort to my soul that I was always searching for but never found, not even in the rarest and most remote places on this earth. Her presence shakes my soul and body, giving me thrills I could only hope to find on my explorations. From the moment we met, something deep within me stirred and I knew she would be my greatest adventure. I am ready now to spend the rest of my life learning her and loving her. My soul resonates with hers and we make a song more beautiful than any bird could sing and a light show more spectacular than the lights in the northernmost sky. Our lives are forever entwined. I am hers and she is mine, from now through all eternity. I am ready.

Benji's eyes hung on the line that talked about the song and lights. He read it a few more times and then looked up at Jay.

"Do you think that Edwina and this Aimee were like us?"

Jay had already pulled out another book and opened it to a page that showed an article from an early paper with an obituary of "the spectacular Aimee Ottmisse," an aural who used her talents to paint images based on the colors she saw in the world around her. She had been hired to paint Edwina's portrait for some explorer's guild hall of fame and the two had apparently hit it off. The article said they went on to be best friends and old women who lived together until the end of their days, as they were both unmarried.

"So they were 'roommates' and 'best friends,' then?" Benji asked, stifling a laugh.

"Sure. Same as we are," Jay agreed.

They burst into giggles. Benji would never tire of

hearing Jay's infectious laughter. Benji's aura might have started as gold, but Jay's laugh was the true treasure.

"I have another theory to research, but how much do you know of your family tree?" Jay asked Benji.

"Umm, not a lot. My dad's grandfather was adopted, and he never found any information about his birth parents. Why?"

"Well..." Jay snagged another diary from his bag and opened it. This one was covered in paints and color. "It's Aimee's."

Benji read the entry Jay had opened to out loud.

"I have met the most wonderful color. She is a rich burgundy and her color contains multitudes. There are fractals of color and light that dance within. I have seen her color call out to mine when we passed in close proximity as if it was trying to draw mine in and blend it to a new hue. With my gold and her burgundy, we would make a fire so intense I would have to look away from its brightness and radiance."

Jay flipped the page to a much later entry and Benji continued.

"I am grateful that my dearest Edwina has traversed the globe and seen many things. It meant when I revealed my true nature to her, she was undisturbed and instead insisted that she loved me all the more because I had unearthed my secret to her. She is unconcerned about my anatomy and instead has dedicated most of her days to worshipping it. She has brought me the utmost bliss and when I am within her, our souls sing in harmony."

Benji pulled the diary into his lap.

"Do you think Aimee was a trans woman?" He asked.

"I do," Jay admitted. "But more than that, Benj, I think she might have been your ancestor. I think you are a direct descendent of Edwina and Aimee. Edwina's obituary mentioned her having a ward who lived with them. I think the ward was their child."

Benji sat back, speechless. Jay took the diary from his lap and placed it back in his bag with the others. He placed his arm around Benji and tugged him close to his side. Benji felt overwhelmed with the revelations, but Jay's closeness soothed him. He closed his eyes and took deep breaths, concentrating on Jay's hands running soothing patterns along his arms.

"I cancelled my talk," Jay confessed when Benji's breathing had evened out.

"Why?"

"It wasn't fair to disclose something so soon after finding out this factor of it. It was personal before because it was you and me, but now, there's an added history and familial component to it. I wanted to make sure that you were cared for. And I didn't want to out Aimee. She and Edwina deserve peace. And so do you," Jay explained.

A weight he hadn't even known was there lifted from Benji's chest.

"Thank you," he whispered.

"If you ever decide you want to disclose this, we can, but for now, I'm happy keeping it to the four of us. Well, and Fjona. I'm pretty sure she knows, too, somehow."

"That cat is an enigma."

Jay nodded his head in agreement.

"How is your sculpture coming along?" he asked after a few more minutes of quiet.

"Almost finished. I'm just waiting for it to dry. Do you want to see?" Benji's energy was starting to return as he talked about the Alchvhybium.

"Please." Jay gestured for Benji to take the lead.

Benji got up off the loveseat and stretched to release the tension he had been holding in his body since the revelation about his potential ancestry. He offered his hand out to Jay and smiled when the jolt at their touch made him feel like he was diving. They walked over to the worktable that Benji had draped in a dark light-exclusionary fabric. He pulled it off and revealed the piece.

He watched as Jay walked around it, taking in the onyx, copper, and Alchvhybium that blended together. The outer shell of the Alchvhybium had fully hardened and the blue magma core was starting to move around. Benji paid close attention to Jay's reactions. When he had finally finished examining the piece, he looked over at Benji from across the table and Benji gasped.

The reflection of the sculpture lined up perfectly with the pattern in Jay's heterochromatic eyes. The countless hours he had fruitlessly tried to draw them and here he had created an exact replica.

"What's wrong?" Jay asked, concerned.

"Nothing. It's just. This piece. It's you. Your eyes. I've been trying to figure them out for months and I've had the answer all along. Your eyes, Jay. When I said I've seen them in dreams before, I didn't realize just how long I'd been dreaming of them."

"What are you talking about?"

Benji needed to explain better.

"Come here." He gestured Jay to come to where he was standing. He summoned a mirror from his desk and held it out so Jay could see his own reflection.

"Look at your eyes. Study the shapes, especially in your left eye."

He waited while Jay did that and then lowered the mirror

"Okay, now look at the sculpture from right here," Benji moved Jay over a step until he was properly lined up. Jay looked at the sculpture and his eyes went wide.

"Oh my gods. It's my eye. You are such a romantic."

Benji wrapped his arms around Jay's waist and then gently bit his shoulder.

"What are you going to call it?" Jay asked.

"The sculpture?"

Jay nodded.

"His cosmos, my heart."

"Yup, definitely a romantic."

Jay spun in Benji's arms and kissed him so deeply that Benji was seeing stars.

epilogue

An Apartment in New York City

JAY WOKE up with familiar fingers carding through his hair and a purring weight on his chest.

"Did you enjoy your nap?" his husband asked.

"I did. What did you do while I was out?"

"Mostly this." Benji played with Jay's curls again. "And some daydreaming."

"Anything good?"

"I was thinking about other universes and how I probably have this work issue figured out in one of them. I wish I could just pop over there for the answer and then come back."

"Why come back?" Jay asked.

"Because you're here. And our little Olive princess, too." He reached forward and gave the calico cat a gentle pet.

"You don't think I'd be in that universe?"

Benji thought for a moment. "You probably would, and you'd probably help me in that one, too."

"I would?" Jay glanced up at his husband and gave him a smirk. He tried, and failed, to raise a singular eyebrow which made Benji smile.

"Yeah, and in that one, you can raise your eyebrow successfully."

They both laughed and Jay settled back deeper in Benji's lap. Olive opened a single eye and repositioned herself once Jay had stopped moving. He gave her a few pets as an apology for disturbing her sleep. She chirped her approval.

"So, your problem… Sorry I fell asleep when you were talking about it earlier. What's going on? How can I help?"

Jay listened as Benji described a conflict with one of the processes he was trying to implement for his colleagues, and they spent a good part of the evening problem solving and trying to come up with various solutions.

Benji had a few more ideas to work through by the time they had exhausted their brains. They settled in to watch a movie after cleaning up from dinner. This time, Benji laid with his head in Jay's lap. Olive watched from her throne of a cat tree as they put on a British sci-fi show they loved watching together. This particular episode was the beginning of an arc that was set in a different universe. It set Jay's thoughts back to the conversation they had when he woke up from his nap.

He kept thinking about the existence of a multiverse or at least an alternate universe as they got ready for bed.

"Okay, babe, what's going on in your head? You've been quiet since we settled down after dinner. Are you okay?" Benji asked as he climbed into their bed.

"Yeah, I'm good. I was just thinking about the stuff we talked about earlier."

"For my problem?" Benji opened his arms and Jay got in and snuggled up to his side.

"No, right after my nap, when we were talking about different universes and how things might be parallel, but they're also not the same in every detail."

Benji waited as Jay continued to gather his thoughts.

"I... I just think things aren't always the greatest here, but at least we have each other. I can't imagine a universe where we weren't together."

"Neither can I. I honestly don't think that universe exists. Jay Byrd, I promise I'd find you and fall in love with you in every universe that's out there."

Benji's assurance and accompanying kiss settled his nerves to the point where Jay's brain finally started to calm down. It didn't take long before he started to drift off to sleep again, his husband's vow to always be by his side in every part of the multiverse that might exist keeping him feeling safe and loved.

acknowledgments

A huge thanks to everyone who helped make this possible:

Firstly, to my husband — I love you so much. Thanks for being the most supportive human and partner (and for keeping me fed and hydrated).

Next, to Amy — Thanks for being my cheerleader and for reading through early versions of the Benji and Jay story.

To Cait — Thank you for always letting me bounce my thoughts and ideas off of you.

To Rosie — Thank you for all the notes of encouragement and support throughout the process.

To Bethany — Thanks for being the best bromance buddy this author could ever imagine having. <3

To the Peach Pit — Thank you for being such enthusiastic supporters and enablers.

To Matt — Thank you for all the early advice and words of encouragement.

To the staff of the tea room where I write — Thanks for keeping me going every Tuesday.

To Sarah — Thank you for the check-ins, support, and love. You are my favorite cousin.

To Nina — Thanks for getting me out of my house and keeping me with one foot in the real world so I can continue to dream.

To Queso — Thanks for being a loud nuisance and reminding me to take breaks.

To Taako — Thanks for crying at me to go to bed every night.

To my editor, Lindsey — Thank you firstly for all the extensions (sorry again for those) and for dealing with my chaos. I appreciate you more than words can say.

To my cover artist, Kay — Thank you for bringing Benji and Jay's world to life.

To Casey and the staff at Golden Bee — Thank you for being my safe haven and for letting me spew about everything I have going on.

To my readers — Thanks for taking a chance on this story. I write because I have stories to tell, but those stories would go nowhere without readers to enjoy them. I hope you've enjoyed the introduction to Benji and Jay's multiverse and that you'll come back for more.

And finally, to the band Sub-Radio — Thanks for the song that kicked off this whole idea, "Dimension". Keep being the amazing queer icons and trans allies that you are.

about the author

Pip Dolyn (they/he) is an emerging author of queer and trans romance. The Alchvhybium Bet is their second book.

Pip lives in Central New York with his husband and their two cats, Queso and Taako (yes, from tv).

You can find Pip online at @pipdolynwrites on Instagram and Threads as well as at pipdolyn.com

also by pip dolyn

The Dandelion & the Thistle: Makers Market Book 1

www.ingramcontent.com/pod-product-compliance
Lightning Source LLC
LaVergne TN
LVHW041101150826
845673LV00007B/1877

* 9 7 9 8 9 9 2 1 4 6 3 3 2 *